Heroes of the Blue Sky Rebellion

Healthy Village Press
Halethorpe, Maryland USA

Heroes

of the Blue Sky Rebellion

How You and Other Young Men
Can Claim All the Happiness in the World

Jack Kammer

Stay in touch with the Blue Sky Rebellion at
www.blueskyrebellion.com

Healthy Village Press enriches lives
around the world by reminding human societies
of the importance and inherent worth
of men and boys and how they contribute
to healthy families, communities, towns, cities,
nations and planets.

Healthy Village Press
P.O. Box 18236
Halethorpe MD 21227
USA
information@healthyvillagepress.com

Heroes of the Blue Sky Rebellion
First edition 2009

ISBN: 978-0-578-03066-1
Library of Congress Control Number: 2009931977

The most sexist idea of all is the belief that only one sex is harmed by sexism.

Table of Contents

Acknowledgments

Janet, the healer.

Maria, the teacher.

An ever-growing network of men and women around the world who are committed to fairness and equity between the sexes. Especially Fred Hayward.

J. Steven Svoboda, who read the work in progress and offered essential suggestions.

Miss Porter and Bovina for the fun picture.

My mother for helping me believe in myself. My father for inspiring me to stand up for others.

Preface: Is This Book for You?

This book is for boys and young men age 13 to 23 who sometimes get the feeling that maybe something is not quite right about the way boys and young men are treated, especially compared to how things are for girls and young women.

But it's not only about fairness between the sexes. It's also about what results from lack of fairness. It will help your enjoyment of this book if you are open, for instance, to the possible connection between unfairness to boys and young men on the one hand, and the violence boys and young men perpetrate on the other. Similarly, this book also deals with the problems of educational underachievement, depression, suicide and family strife—all of which might be very real and present in your life or in the life of the community you live in.

There have been many "boy crisis" books that have been written *about* boys and young men and the unhappiness and difficulties you might be facing. Most of those books have been written for adults, to give them ideas about how they can help. But most adults seem not nearly concerned enough with the problems of boys and young men, and not willing to make the changes many boys and young men need.

This book is written *for* boys and young men, to give you ideas you can use as you see fit, by your own choice and under your control. It is not about how to "cope" with the problems of being "a guy," but rather how to fix those problems and put an end to them so that you can spend less energy on coping and more on living your life fully, freely and joyfully.

If you are a go-along-to-get-along type of young man, this book is not for you. It will make you uncomfortable with the suggestions it makes. If you only want to "fit in," you can close this book right now. And no one should criticize you for doing so.

But if you believe or even just have a feeling that there is a side to the story of gender discrimination that still needs to be told, you might enjoy this book a lot.

How Can This Book Help You?

This book can help you in two main ways, both involving more freedom for you.

First: "Freedom from." The Blue Sky Rebellion can help you win freedom from the outmoded rules and mind games that people use to control you because you're male. Most of those mind games are based on making you feel insecure about yourself. And most of the rules are based on sexist biases, prejudices and stereotypes about boys and young men.

Second: "Freedom to." The Blue Sky Rebellion can help you have the freedom to do what you want to do, feel what you really feel, be who you really are, and act as you think best for you and your life. It can bolster your confidence, pride, integrity and optimism about yourself as a male.

In short, this book can help you stay true to yourself, help you make your world a friendlier place and help you prepare for your happy future. All at the same time.

Introduction

On March 11, 2009, President Obama signed an Executive Order creating the White House Council on Women and Girls. "The purpose of this Council," he said, "is to ensure that American women and girls are treated fairly in all matters of public policy."

President Obama took no such action for you.[1]

THE WHITE HOUSE

Office of the Press Secretary

FOR IMMEDIATE RELEASE   March 11, 2009

President Obama Announces White House Council on Women and Girls

President Obama today signed an Executive Order creating the White House Council on Women and Girls. The mission of the Council will be to provide a coordinated federal response to the challenges confronted by women and girls and to ensure that all Cabinet and Cabinet-level agencies consider how their policies and programs impact women and families. The Council will be chaired by Valerie Jarrett, Assistant to the President and Senior Advisor, and will include as members cabinet-level federal agencies.

On April 16, 2009, the *New York Times* told of a sociologist who had extensively interviewed middle school boys in 2003 and 2004. "Boys were showing each other they were tough," the researcher commented. "They were afraid to do anything that might be called girlie. It was just like what I would have found if I had done this research 50 years ago. They were frozen in time."[2]

Girls have been anything but frozen over the past half-century and they are thriving in many new and positive ways. It's as if the last forty-five years have been one long, enthusiastic pep rally for girls, telling them they can be and do anything they want, while boys have been pretty much ignored—or even cheered against.

> "My daughters and all of your daughters will forever know that there is no barrier to who they are and what they can be in the United States of America. They can take for granted that women can do anything that the boys can do—and do it better."
>
> —*Barack Obama in Unity, New Hampshire*
> *June 27, 2008*[3]

So maybe our society has some catching up to do in treating you fairly and giving you equal respect, freedom and options in your life. Maybe one day soon a U.S. President will be able to say, "My sons and all of your sons will forever know that there is no barrier to who they are and what they can be in the United States of America. They can take for granted that boys and men can do anything that girls and women can do—and do it just as well."

You might want to view the video at blueskyrebellion.com. For the most part, it's a multimedia version of this Introduction.

What Is the Blue Sky Rebellion?

The Blue Sky Rebellion right now is what the modern Women's Movement was in 1840.

The Blue Sky Rebellion right now is what the Civil Rights Movement was in 1947.

The Blue Sky Rebellion right now is what the Gay Liberation Movement was in 1968.

The Blue Sky Rebellion right now is not much. It is only an idea.

What the Blue Sky Rebellion becomes depends on what you and your young male friends make of it.

This is the idea:

You and other young men are in some ways severely restricted in who and how you can be. Those restrictions are based on old and unnecessary stereotypes very much like the ones that operated against the freedom and happiness of women, African-Americans and gays. (Have you ever wanted or needed to say or do something, but you couldn't because it would have been considered "weak" or "punk"?)

You and your male peers are often victims of discrimination motivated and rationalized by biases and bigotry, much like the bigoted, selfish ideas that allowed women, African-Americans and gays to be mistreated. (Have you ever seen a boy and a girl do something "bad" together, while it is the boy who is more severely blamed and punished?)

Adult men, for reasons we will talk about later, have been unable to launch and sustain a meaningful movement to help you. So it is up to you and your friends to talk candidly about the problems in your life that require change. It is up to you to make sure those changes happen.

The Blue Sky Rebellion is only an idea. But it might also be one of the most powerful forces on earth—an idea whose time has come: a social movement of boys and young men to identify and address the ways sexism operates against you.

The name of the Blue Sky Rebellion comes from the following fable.

A Tale of One Island:
How the Blue Sky Rebellion Began

Once, in the ocean near the equator, there was an island with a mountain range running down the middle and rocky cliffs almost all the way around. The eastern half was wet and green. The western side was hard and dry, and it sloped down to a beach, the one spot on the island that allowed easy access to the sea. Two tribes lived here. The Land People farmed the rainy side. The Sea People fished in the ocean.

Each tribe secretly thought it was better than the other. "We grow things that are sweet and delicious," the Land People boasted. "We produce flowers just because they're beautiful. We create life. The Sea People only kill things by hauling them out of the water to die."

"We provide protein from the ocean," the Sea People said, "and protein is what muscles are made of. We risk our lives by venturing into the open sea." Young Sea People had to show they were strong and fearless and they had to learn songs about "The Dangers of the Deep Blue Sea" and "The Endless Power of the Big Blue Sky."

The Sea People installed barriers along the mountain ridge to keep Land People out. The Land People quietly protected their half by putting pink wherever they could; they knew that Sea People avoided pink.

One day a few Land People said they wanted to go across the mountains to the beach and catch their own fish. They could help the island have more fish, they said, and they would like to do something new.

At first almost everyone on both sides of the island opposed the idea. But eventually the rules changed, the Sea People's mountaintop barriers came down, and soon Land People were fishing in the ocean.

When the Sea People took their fish to the market in the middle of the island the Land People said, "We catch our own fish now. Instead of five tomatoes for each fish, we'll give you two."

The Sea People got very upset, but they couldn't say anything. Since Sea People all acted like fish were the most important food, why would any Sea Person get upset about a couple of stupid tomatoes? Or corn? Or strawberries? Or...?

Tensions rose between the two tribes. Since Sea People had the reputation for being stronger and—now—*angrier!*, they were almost always the ones who were blamed whenever there was trouble. Sea People were fighting more among themselves, too. Some young Sea People grew so sad they jumped off the cliffs into the sea to end their lives.

The Sea People elders paid no attention until the Land People started to complain. "Your young Sea People are out of control! We need more rules! They're so angry! Have you heard the songs they're singing about Land People? How disrespectful!"

The Sea People elders told each other, "Young Sea People need more blue in their lives! They don't sing the songs about the Deep Blue Sea and the Big Blue Sky! Let's sing like we did in the old days before the Land People came to our beach! 'Blue, Blue, my life is Blue…'"

But it didn't work. Young Sea People started talking about the problem to their most trusted friends. Without actually saying so, some let it be known that they were secretly growing plants—and it made them feel good. They wondered why they couldn't go to the other side of the island where growing things was easier. They said they liked blue, but they didn't think pink was all that disgusting. They were happy to learn that lots of other young Sea People felt the same way. They decided, whether the elders liked it or not, that things were going to change.

Word spread fast. At midnight, a crowd of young Sea People started over the mountains. As daylight began to break, they saw pink just about everywhere, but it didn't bother them a bit.

Soon they got to the first Land People village, where a Land People elder was blocking the path. "Hold it right there!" she commanded. "You are not welcome here. We know of your violent, angry ways. We live in peace. We do not kill. We need protection from the likes of you."

"But wait," one of the young Sea People said. "We like to grow things, just like you do."

"We trust you not! If you want to be here," the Land People elder demanded, "you must renounce all things blue!"

"No! We like blue," the young Sea Person said. "We just don't want everything in our lives to be all blue all the time."

Just then, the Sea People elders came rushing down the path. "Turn around and march home right this instant!" they ordered. "We don't belong here. This land is not our land. We didn't come here when we were growing up and—look at us!—we turned out just fine! You must renounce all this silly pinkness!"

"No!" the young Sea Person leader exclaimed. "Didn't you always tell us about the Endless Power of the Big Blue Sky? Well, look," he said pointing eastward toward the rising sun. "There's plenty of Big Blue Sky out there, just as there is in the west. And the pink of the sunrise only makes it all the more beautiful. It's a new day. We're taking control of our own lives. We renounce nothing!"

Principles of The Blue Sky Rebellion

1. The Blue Sky Rebellion will make the world better for everyone.

2. One of the best ways to make the world better for everyone is to make sure that you and your young male friends feel happy, healthy, fairly treated and appreciated.

3. While traditional sex roles and gender expectations impose disadvantages on girls and young women, they also provide advantages.

4. While traditional sex roles and gender expectations provide advantages to you and your young male friends, they also impose disadvantages.

5. There are many negative stereotypes and biases about girls and young women. Girls and young women have benefited greatly from overcoming those ideas and the policies they generated.

6. There are many negative stereotypes and biases about you and your young male friends. You will benefit greatly from overcoming those ideas and the policies they generate.

7. You and your young male friends deserve the right to choose how you want to live your lives, with as many options for fulfillment and happiness as girls and young women enjoy.

8. You and your young male friends deserve as much love, affection, compassion and respect as girls and young women receive.

9. Change is difficult—especially for people who feel powerful with the world as it is—and nobody gives up power willingly…unless they get something better in return. It is therefore up to us to demonstrate the truth of Principle Number One.

You Deserve Better

> "Well, for one thing, the culture we have does not make people feel good about themselves. We're teaching the wrong things. And you have to be strong enough to say if the culture doesn't work, don't buy it. Create your own. Most people can't do it."
>
> *Morrie Schwartz*[4]

Most young men between 13 and 23 are doing okay. But things could be better. Much better. Some young men, as you probably know, are not feeling so good. Some are angry, some are depressed, some are cynical. Even the young men who are doing "okay" could use some changes. They have to use precious time and energy to overcome and deal with problems that result only from old-fashioned and pointless ideas about how boys and young men "should" be.

We're going to look closely at those problems. Our purpose isn't to get negative, cynical and depressed, but rather to get excited, energetic and determined about moving the problems out of the way so you can be happier and healthier now and for the rest of your life.

Some people think that you need to change, that boys are too, well, male. These people don't like the way boys are; they want boys to be more like girls.

You young men and boys don't need to change; we adults need to put a stop to all the things that try to change you in the first place, all the forces that try to keep you from being all the great and wonderful things you and other young men naturally are.[5]

Sexism? Against Boys?

In kindergarten, Jessica likes to play with the toy saw and hammer and that's just fine. Jason likes to play with the miniature kitchen appliances but the adults in his life let him know he really shouldn't.

In elementary school, Jessica wears a T-shirt saying "Girls rule. Boys drool," and that's considered empowerment. Jason is overheard saying to a friend that girls are dumb in math and he's sent to the principal's office because that's considered harassment.

In middle school, Jessica attends a special girls-only science and math program to help and encourage her to keep up with boys in those subjects[6]; Jason lags behind girls in reading and writing, but there are no programs to encourage or inspire him and his friends with the same problem. He grows nervous and fidgety in class because he can't keep up. He gets medicated.

In high school, Jessica tells her friend, "You go, girl!" Jason tells his friend, "Boy, don't go there!"

In a classic experiment, two scientists made a videotape of a crying nine-month-old infant and showed it to adult men and women. The scientists told some of the grown-ups that the baby was a boy, and they told the others it was a girl. The adults who thought they were watching a crying boy were more likely to say "he" was "angry." The adults who thought the crying baby was a girl were more likely to say "she" was "frightened."[7] It's not too hard to imagine that adults treat "angry" children differently from how they treat "frightened" children, is it? Adults will probably be nicer to frightened children than they are to angry ones. Does that make you think that maybe girls automatically get nicer treatment than boys do? Hmmmmm…Sexism against males?

> "[Being a boy] means that your actions are more likely to be misinterpreted as threatening or disobedient, that you are more likely than the girl next door to be punished or treated harshly…Judges commit boys to juvenile detention centers more often than they commit girls, even when the offense is the same."
>
> *Dan Kindlon and Michael Thompson*[8]

Fair Shake?

We can see that boys in general aren't performing and achieving so well these days—they aren't going to college[9, 10, 11], they are getting into trouble[12], they are quitting school[13]. What is going on? What can help?

In 2008 a researcher in Europe put pairs of dogs side-by-side and asked them to "shake" (raise their paws as if to shake hands). When both dogs were given treats, they both raised their paws as requested nearly every time. When neither dog was given a treat they cooperated 20 out of 30 times. But when only one dog was given a treat, the unrewarded dog cooperated only 12 out of 30 times and showed considerable agitation at the inequity.[14]

Unfairness to boys, though seldom discussed, might help explain why boys often feel agitated. Everyone wants to feel appreciated and accepted, boys and young men included—even, and perhaps especially, the ones who act like they don't really care. When boys and young men don't get those good feelings of acceptance, respect and belonging they often get angry, act out or give up. And getting shamed for being male makes boys' alienation only worse[15], especially when all around them they see girls being praised and encouraged just for being girls.

It's one thing when a renegade rap artist says ugly and mean things about girls. It's quite another when the paternalistic and benevolent, mainstream, All-American, wholesome Disney movie studio shows ugly and mean things being done to boys. In 1995, Disney made *Tom and Huck*, a movie based on Mark Twain's books about Tom Sawyer and Huckleberry Finn. Disney included two scenes that say a lot about the mean, anti-boy spirit of our time.

Here, Becky Thatcher, with no justification whatsoever, pushes Tom from a bridge into a stream. Isn't that *funny*?

Okay, so maybe that's not such a big deal. But here is Becky slugging Tom in the face after he falls through the ceiling of the church at what was supposed to be his funeral.

There is absolutely no basis in Mark Twain's books for either of these incidents, but Disney figured that audiences would like them. In fact, Disney thought these scenes would be such crowd-pleasers that it put both of them in the movie's preview trailer. Did you see Becky slug Tom? You go girl! It's also worth noting that Disney had Becky spitting indignantly at Tom, "Don't tell me what to do!" when he very rightly tried to keep her quiet to avoid worsening a cave-in. Oh, we just love seeing boys put down, don't we?

Do People Really Even Care About the Problems You Face As a Young Male?

Did you know that significantly more boys than girls are fatally abused by their parents and caregivers?[16] Have you ever heard anyone talk about that? To make public inattention to this issue worse, on December 31, 2000, the *Washington Post* reported that 115 girl babies and 158 boy babies were killed in the U.S. in 1997, but used a headline saying "A Case of Little Girls Dying."[17] Thirty-seven percent more boys than girls were killed, but the story focused on the girls. Strange!

In 1933, in the 15-24 age group, the rate of suicide for males was 1.54 times higher than for females. That means for every 100 young women who killed themselves in 1933 (the height of the Great Depression, when jobs and money were very scarce), about 154 young men did the same. Seventy-three years later, in 2006 (during relatively good economic times), the last year for which complete statistics are available, the male rate was 5.04 times higher than the female rate[18]. That means for every 100 young women who killed themselves in 2006, about 504 young men did the same. The suicide imbalance between the sexes more than tripled in seventy-three years.[19]

As with the fatal abuse of boys, the media give precious little attention to male suicide. While covering a rash of "youth" suicides in South Boston, NBC News on May 6, 1997 never mentioned that *all* the victims were male. Neither did NPR's "Weekend All Things Considered," covering the same story on June 15, 1997.

8

In 2006, the director of the American Association of Suicidology told a newspaper reporter, "As much as I would love to lead the charge (in finding out why boys kill themselves), try to go out and get funding for it." The reporter noted, "[the director] is frustrated that funders aren't interested in studying boys and men…The association has an expert on female suicide but none on male suicide."[20] In May 2009, the National Association of Social Workers launched its SHIFT program "to make a change in the alarming suicide statistics for adolescent girls."[21] Social workers and their funders have not seen fit to do anything similar to stem the much higher number of suicides among adolescent boys.

For every boy who kills himself how many others are suffering silently, feeling ashamed and unworthy of help?

The news is not all bad. There have been multiple good books (see the Bibliography, page 96) and magazine articles (notably *Newsweek*'s January 30, 2006 cover story by Peg Tyre on "The Boy Crisis") about the problems you face as a young male. But with large social institutions—from the White House on down—largely ignoring the problems you face as a young man, we have a lot of work to do.

It is good to note that much-needed attention is being paid to the especially difficult circumstances of many African-American young men and boys. But that attention almost always focuses on racial discrimination and not at all on how antimale biases and sexism operate against young Black males.[22]

Along the same lines it's important to mention that many state and local juvenile justice systems around the nation offer gender-specific programs for girls who have broken the law, but one of the nation's leading experts on gender-specific juvenile justice programming said she knows of no such programs for criminally involved boys.[23, 24, 25]

Boys Gotta Be Tough

An expert on how to raise daughters wrote "We're open and gentle with girls because we don't get caught up in silliness about making them tough, like we do with sons."[26] Here's a grown-up admitting that at least some adults, perhaps most adults, are not open and gentle with boys.

Why does society want or need to treat boys harshly? What good does it do, why is it necessary or productive? What problem does it solve?

The reason might be that society has a pretty hard, unattractive job it needs us boys and men to do and it has to use whatever tricks it can to get us to do it. It can't be too concerned with our feelings. In fact, it even convinces itself that we don't really even have feelings. And if it sees any evidence that we really do have feelings, it shames us for showing them. How dare we make them see the falseness of their idea!

Furthermore, feelings only get in the way of doing your job. In essence the traditional male job is to compete and produce. When you have to view other people as adversaries or obstacles to your success, you'll never survive if you care about them, if you don't stomp out your feelings of empathy and compassion.[27] So, lo and behold, society actually gets to feel like it's doing us a favor by ignoring our feelings. It's helping to toughen us up so we can "succeed."

> The Darwinian notion of "survival of the fittest" is stressful, especially for males, upon whom the primary obligation falls for being victorious in fighting and other physical competitions for safety and scarce resources. But one thing that is often missed in discussions of Darwinism is that being social and able to cooperate is as much an element of fitness for human survival as the ability to compete. As males we need to demand that attentiveness to intimate relationships and our ability to cooperate and build consensus are not mistaken for weakness or unmanliness.[28, 29]

Get Hitched

Males function a little like beasts of burden.[30] In at least one important way, men are like oxen, hitched to a cart in which women and children are riding. Indeed, one of the slang expressions in male culture for marriage is "getting hitched," like an animal being tied to a wagon. That's not the only thing getting married is like, of course. There can be plenty of good things about it. But the fact that this term exists is evidence that a lot of men see their role as a restriction and a burden rather than a joy and an opportunity.

Society knows that if it gave boys a choice, if it gave you the chance to really, really decide for yourself how you want to live your life, you might look at the typical male role and say "Thanks, but no thanks."

That might be the biggest reason why society wants to control you more strictly and give you fewer choices than girls and young women have.

So Few Choices. So Much Time.

Imagine asking 100 boys and 100 girls which of the following options they think realistically they would be able to take for themselves in their adult lives:

- work full-time all your adult life until you retire
- work full-time until you have children, then stay home with the kids full-time until they start school
- work full-time until you have children, then work part-time so you can stay home with the kids part-time
- work full-time until you have children, stay home with the kids full-time until they start high school, then go back to work full-time
- work full-time until you have children, stay home with the kids full-time until they start high school, then go back to work part-time.
- marry a rich person, have no kids and stay home to pursue creative endeavors like writing or painting, or performing volunteer work.

Based on what we know about gender roles and expectations today, we might expect that almost all of the 100 boys would answer yes to the first choice and that not very many boys would answer yes to the other possibilities. And we might expect that almost all of the hundred girls would answer yes multiple times, they could see themselves possibly embracing just about all those options at some point in their lives—depending on whom they marry, of course. Notice that for girls and women to have so many choices, it's necessary for boys and men to have few. The family cart has to be pulled.

A daytime talk show was on the TV in the waiting room of an auto shop where I was having some work done on my car. The topic was "Men Who Stay Home With Their Kids." When the burly mechanic came to tell me my car was ready, he stopped to watch. "What do you think of that?" I asked, fully expecting him to say something about child rearing not being "real man's work." "I'd love to do that," he answered, "but my wife took that job. She didn't even ask. She just took it."

In his book *I Don't Want To Talk About It*, Terrence Real tells a story about his family: "My father...worked his way through [art school]. Sculpture...was his great passion. But my father had three hungry people to care for, and so he switched his major from fine art to industrial design. Years later, he told me that a part of him had died on the day he went to the registrar's office to make the change."[31]

Have things changed? In 2001 writer Cathy Young observed, "In one couple I know, the father had to drop out of a graduate program in music when he learned that a baby was on the way; he finds his current corporate job boring and exhausting and hates the long hours away from his son. The mother, who quit an office job she never much liked, seems to be enjoying her time at home. Who's making the sacrifice?"[32]

Yes, things have changed, but primarily for the benefit of girls and young women. They need to change for the good of boys and young men, too.[33]

Girls Yes. Boys No.

In January 2000, *Parade* magazine columnist Marilyn Vos Savant conducted a poll on readers' attitudes about choices and options for sons and daughters. She received 7,758 responses to these two questions:

1. Should we teach our daughters that they have a choice between having a career and staying at home?
   • 83 percent of the men said yes; 17 percent said no.
   • 77 percent of the women said yes; 23 percent said no.
2. Should we teach our sons that they have a choice between having a career and staying at home?
   • 28 percent of the men said yes; 72 percent said no.
   • 40 percent of the women said yes; 60 percent said no.

The *Parade* poll is not a scientific, statistically representative survey, but its results have been borne out by studies that are.[34] We have good reason to conclude that society doesn't want boys to have the same choices girls have.

Some people will say, "What boy would even want to stay home and raise his kids? Boys don't want to do that!" And they will point to the fact that so few men are staying home to be full-time parents.

People who say that should be reminded that forty-five years ago other people said, "What girl would even want to go to law school? Girls don't want to do that!" And they pointed to the fact that there were very few women applying to law school. And they quoted the law school admissions directors who said, "We absolutely don't discriminate against females. Females just don't apply. Apparently they don't want to be lawyers. In fact, we accept a higher percentage of female applicants than male applicants." (The admissions office didn't mention that he received two applications from females and accepted one of them.) The point, of course, is that when girls didn't know they could go to law school, when they were told they weren't smart or logical enough to go to law school or be successful lawyers, when they thought they wouldn't be welcome in law school or law offices, when they weren't encouraged to pursue their interests and get ready for law school, when they thought that good, healthy, respectable women didn't go to law school, then—no surprise!—they didn't go to law school. Now, of course, women go to law school in great numbers. In fact, in the 2007-2008 school year they were 47.3 percent of all first year law school enrollments.[35]

By the same token, until you and other young men know for certain that you have everything you need to be successful as full and equal parents, that you will be welcomed in that pursuit, that women will value you for things other than being "Good Providers," that our laws respect fathers as much as mothers if and when there is a divorce, few young men will dream of or plan on devoting themselves to parenthood the way women know they can. It is not unusual to hear stories of full-time, stay-at-home fathers who are shunned by mothers at the playground and regarded with disdain by men at their wives' company parties. It is also true that many women want fathers to be better assistants, but not fully, truly equal parents.[36] All of that needs to change. You and other Blue Sky Rebels can help to change it.

On Your Mark! Get Set! Go Where?

We hear a lot about how you as a male have unfair advantages over females because of all the great jobs you'll have and all the money you'll make. But let's look deeper.

Imagine you're in a race from New York to LA and the rules give you a headstart by letting you start in Cleveland. That's a big advantage, isn't it? Yes, but only if you want to go to LA. What if you have no choice? What if you don't care about this race? What if where you really want to go is London or Sydney or Kinshasa or Paris or Tokyo or Istanbul? At what point does an "advantage" become an obligation? It's like society gives boys and young men a free coupon…for something many boys and young men don't really want. To make matters worse, the coupon comes with the expectation that you won't "waste" it and will go out and buy the standard male role that society is selling, whether you want it or not.

Think of it like this: Suppose your father wants you to be a professional baseball player, but you don't really want to be one at all. If he goes out and buys you a brand new glove, is that a present or a pressure? A gift or a burden? An advantage or an obligation?

And if everyone believes you've had a headstart in the money-making race and you end up making only as much money as a female who hasn't had that supposed advantage, you're really "a loser," aren't you? And if you should make less...? The pressure is on!

Don't Men Run the World?

"Wait!" you might be thinking. "Why would males set up a system that isn't good for them? Don't men run the world? Look at all the people in Congress, look at the president, look at all the big executives!"

Yes, but there's a huge difference between saying "Men have all the power" and "Some men have a lot of power." After all, over whom do the powerful men exert their power? It isn't just women and girls. The Old Boys Club, in which powerful men look out for their buddies, is a reality, but it's also true that most men and boys never become members. And the Old Boys are much more interested in helping non-member females than they are in helping non-member males.

> "In my house, being raised with a sister and three brothers, there was an absolute—a nuclear—sanction if under any circumstances, for any reason, no matter how justified—even self-defense—if you ever touched our sister, literally, not figuratively, literally. My sister...grew up with absolute impunity in our household...and I have the bruises to prove it. And I mean that sincerely. I'm not exaggerating when I say that."
>
> *—Vice President Joseph Biden*
> *December 11, 1990, when he was a Senator*
> *during Judiciary Committee Hearings on*
> *the Violence Against Women Act,*
> *which he has called his "proudest legislative achievement"*[37]

And just about any father who's been through a divorce can tell you that laws aren't always written to help men. Politicians can count. They're especially good at counting votes. They know that women vote on women's issues. They know that men don't often vote on men's issues. (Maybe you and your Rebel allies can change that one day.)

Besides, many of life's most fundamental and pervasive rules aren't from laws passed by legislatures. They're from cultural traditions that both men and women help to shape. Most places don't have laws, for instance, that say that men pay for dates, but we feel compelled to do it nonetheless.[38] (Maybe you can change that too.)

Aren't Girls and Women Stuck Riding in the Cart?

"Wait!" you might be thinking. "If men get stuck pulling the cart, doesn't that mean women are stuck riding in the cart, always with the kids, always dependent on their ox for getting anywhere?"

Yes, girls and women were traditionally limited. No doubt about it.

The difference is that the women's movement has made sure girls have lots of options they never had in the past. If they want to get out and pull a cart or do any of the other rewarding things that some men have been able to do, they're now much more free to give it a go. New options have not been granted nearly so much to you and your young male friends. Change needs to be a two-way street.

Aren't Girls and Women "Oppressed"?

"Wait!" you might be thinking. "We've been hearing for years that women and girls are oppressed!"

Yes, women and girls complain about sexism; men and boys don't. But who is more likely to register a complaint: a rich guest in a luxury hotel who feels the air conditioner is not working exactly right, or a poor migrant farm worker trying to sleep in a steamy bunkhouse with a broken fan? The rich hotel guest complains because she feels entitled. The poor farm worker stays quiet because he has no power to complain. Sometimes a complaint tells us more about the expectations of the complainer than the actual circumstances the complainer is in.[39]

In 2006, researchers investigated the balance of power in young heterosexual couples. They found that boys and girls agreed that the girls have more power, with power defined in terms of this very important question: "If the two of you disagree, who usually gets their way?"[40] If girls usually get their way, can they say they are oppressed?

If we want to use the term "oppressed," maybe the most accurate thing to say is that girls and young women are oppressed and boys and young men are oppressed too. We've heard a lot about the oppression of girls and young women. The Blue Sky Rebellion will bring attention to the ways oppression operates against you and your friends.

Free to Be You, But Not to Be Me

The most important difference between men and women, boys and girls these days is that girls and women have far more choice, far many more options about what they can be and do than boys and men have. Barbie can be anything. GI Joe is still a soldier.

Boy-friendly psychologist William Pollack tells the story of a four-year-old boy named Benjamin who wanted to "play the mother and put on jewelry in the dress-up corner." His pre-school teacher had degrees in early childhood education from Wellesley and Harvard, two of the best and most "progressive" colleges in the nation. Even so, she was worried about Benjamin. She told Pollack that Benjamin cried when she tried to get him to stop and do other things but that "he seems perfectly healthy otherwise." Pollack pointed out to this young teacher that one of her girl students was wearing a cowboy hat and acting like a cowboy. "Sure," the teacher said, "but all the girls do that."[41]

Poor little Benjamin might spend the rest of his life obsessing about jewelry and dress-up—and feeling guilty and weird for doing so.

Picture This

Here we have photographs of two Blue Sky Rebel boys having fun with costumes. In one picture they are following traditional scripts for maleness: they're tough and serious. In the other they are pretending to be something traditionally reserved for the "opposite sex"—Roaring Twenties Flappers—flashy and frivolous.

Who Is Having More Fun?

Does the picture of the boys dressed as women make you uncomfortable somehow? Does it make you feel any better to learn that these are really two regular, non-rebellious girls doing what we allow girls to do all the time? If so, why does it make you feel better? Why is it okay for girls to dress as men, but not for boys to dress as women?

The answer goes back to something we talked about earlier: society can't let men have a choice. If you got to choose the kind of rich, flexible lives that women can have, you might never choose the rigid, often joyless lives society wants men to accept. If you got to stay home and take care of your children, for instance, you might not be so willing to go out to work in a factory or an office.

> "No developing society that needs men to leave home and do 'their thing' for the society ever allows young men in to handle or touch their newborns. There's always a taboo against it. For they know that, if they did, the new fathers would become so hooked they would never get out and do 'their thing' properly."
>
> —*anthropologist Margaret Mead*[42]

As the women's movement has said, the role of women was traditionally "devalued." That was bad for women in one way because it meant women often did not get the economic respect they deserved. But it was good for women in another way because it meant they could spend their lives pretty much as they wanted; since their roles weren't considered worth much, society didn't really care if women deviated from them.

But the other side of the coin is that men's work is overvalued. That was good for men in one way because it meant men were usually respected economically and that respect often translated into good pay. But it was bad in another way because it meant society made sure that men accounted carefully for every bit of their potential value and didn't "waste" any of it on feelings or fun or frivolity that didn't produce anything society wanted or needed economically.

> *Important vs. Powerful vs. Empowered*
>
> In a car, the engine would be considered "more important" than the stereo. But which would be granted its choice, a stereo that wanted to ride along under the hood for a while or an engine that wanted to sit in the back seat and take it easy in the air conditioning for an hour or two?
>
> Being important and powerful doesn't always mean you're empowered to do what you want. Sometimes it just means you have to work harder.

Society doesn't want you to think about the limitations it places on you. It wants you to think your place in the world is glorious. It wants you to think that "it's a man's world!" In some ways it is. In some ways it isn't. The women's movement has talked a lot about the ways it is. The Blue Sky Rebellion will talk about the ways it isn't.[43]

Overcrowding

As girls and women get more and more freedom, boys and young men get more and more crowded into traditional male space. Since being a man supposedly means not being a woman—not "soft," not "weak," not "sissy"—we cram ourselves up against the farthest limits of our territory so we can "prove" we are nowhere near being female.[44] The result is more strife and conflict among ourselves, more distance from what we really want to do, more disconnection from who we really want to be, and more trouble with the power structure that seeks to confine, limit and control us.[45]

We need more space and more freedom of movement. And that brings us to our mission.

The Mission

Our Mission is to gain for boys and young men as much access to traditionally female territory as girls and young women have gained in traditionally male territory. That territory isn't physical. It's not about land and acres. It's emotional, psychological, social, legal and cultural territory.

The Mission is to observe, identify, confront, and disable—nicely, if possible, but firmly as required—sexism, bias and discrimination against boys and young men wherever they occur.

It isn't about turning the clock backward to the old days. It isn't a "backlash" against the gains of women and girls. It's a "frontlash." It's about pushing forward to a world in which "equality" is truly equal. It's about balance, respect, fairness, freedom and full opportunity for everyone.

The Blue Sky Rebellion will:
- expand the concept of "manliness" so you can more comfortably and confidently find your place within it
- gain for you the same life options that girls and women have
- bring you the services and programs you need to succeed in school and other fields of endeavor
- provide balance to public understanding of how power is shared and used between the sexes
- reduce or eliminate the gender discrimination that often causes you to be judged and treated worse than girls and more harshly than you deserve.

Your Natural Allies Have Gone AWOL and MIA (Away Without Leave and Missing in Action)

Back in the 1960s, girls faced similar problems: society held lots of sexist ideas about females. Their roles were narrowly defined. They were regarded as incapable of things we now know they can accomplish just fine. You can take heart from seeing how well girls have succeeded in getting the options and freedom they need and deserve.

But girls were fortunate to have grown women fighting for them. Adult men haven't done much at all to put an end to sexism against you. And, except for a few men in a small and struggling men's movement, it doesn't look like they're anywhere near being ready.

Grown men have a lot of trouble being honest with each other about the fact that being male is often not so great. It's embarrassing to ask other men to join you in solving a mutual problem when you've been raised to think your main relationship with other men should be competition.[46] The fact that they're supposed to believe "It's a man's world" and "Men have all the power" only silences men all the more from acknowledging their problems forthrightly and dealing with them truthfully. They can't talk about your problems with being male if they can't talk about their own.

It's also true that for all their bravado, many adult men are simply afraid to enter into serious, heartfelt discussions and negotiations with women. (No doubt male shame, depression and exhaustion also contribute to adult men's inaction.) Since they can't admit to themselves and their friends that they are actually behaving quite timidly, they have to pretend that the issues at stake aren't really worth worrying about. The result: the difficulties and unfairnesses you face as a boy or young man are downplayed and minimized: "It's no big deal! Get over it! You're whining!" So you get very little help. (And perhaps at some level you get demoralized about the idea of growing up to be a man like that.)

Some men will, in fact, adamantly oppose the Blue Sky Rebellion on the grounds that sexism operates only against females. These fellows will want to talk with you about the omnipotent evils of The Patriarchy—the idea that the world is dominated selfishly by males for males and that females have no power of their own.

There are two possible reasons why the idea of the all-powerful Patriarchy is so adamantly believed by some people. The first is that we do indeed live in a society dominated selfishly and completely by males for males. The other possibility is that we live under a different kind of rule that is so strong and so pervasive that it keeps us from recognizing it for what it really is. The men who harp on The Patriarchy don't see—or can't bring themselves to acknowledge—The Sisterhood, the powerful female union of which virtually every girl and woman is a member.

> "The Sisterhood…dictates that in the battle between the sexes, women friends stick by each other. Men know that when the Sisterhood unites, there will be no peace until they've given up, given in or apologized."
>
> — *Olivette Orme*[47]

Some grown men are clear about what's really going on and will want to help you. And some women will help, too. But mainly you're on your own, at least to start. You've probably seen movies about heroic young people who do courageous and important things without adult help. This is your chance to do it for real.

o o o

Now we're going to talk about Self-defense so you can fend off people who attack you for joining the Blue Sky Rebellion. Don't get discouraged. Later we'll talk about our many possible allies.

Self-defense

> "First they ignore you, then they ridicule you, then they fight you, then you win."
>
> —*Mahatma Gandhi*

From the Fictional Island to Your Real World

The end of "A Tale of One Island" at the beginning of this book was not really the end. It was only the beginning. It's not likely that all the people who gathered around the Rebels at the bottom of the mountain path simply said, "Oh. Okay." There was still a lot of work to do, a lot of resistance to overcome. And so it is in your real life. We will face lots of opponents. And they will attack.

Identifying the Opposition

Lots of people—male and female—will want the Blue Sky Rebellion to go away. They either won't care about or will actively oppose your effort to secure more emotional, psychological, social, legal and cultural territory in which you can live your life fully and happily.

Here are the types of people you can expect will give you a hard time.

1. *People who generally just don't like change.*
2. *People—primarily other young men—whose main concern is trying to "fit in."*
3. *Boys and men who have found some measure of success in traditional male territory and who are uncertain of being able to maintain their current status if the game changes.*
4. *Grown men who don't want to admit that they've been duped or mistreated in their lives.*
5. *People who think girls and women are naturally superior to boys and men.*
6. *Girls and women who know they enjoy significant advantages as a result of sexism against boys and men and don't want to lose those advantages (or even share them).*

But here is the opponent who will fight hardest against the Blue Sky Rebellion:

7. *Advertisers who want to sell you stuff.*

Advertisers don't want you to be happy. They want to make you think either 1) the world is an unhappy, hostile place and you need their products to make it less unhappy and less unsafe, or 2) the world is a wonderfully safe and happy place and everyone is having a great time, so what's the matter with you? What's the matter with you, of course, is that you haven't bought (enough of) what they're selling. Look at all the happy people in their commercials!

Advertisers can't sell you Honor, Honesty, Courage, Commitment, Responsibility, Altruism, Decency, Compassion or Diligence and they have no reason to let you think those things are anywhere near as important as what they can sell you: clothes, cars, energy drinks and other things of little lasting value or consequence. In fact, they'd like to convince you that choosing their brand of basketball shoe is the most meaningful commitment you can make in your whole life.

Advertisers want to get into your head (and your wallet) the quickest and most effective way they can. They want to push the most powerful buttons they can find—your young male insecurities, especially about sex, "manliness" and coolness. And not only will they keep hitting you on your insecurities, they'll also do whatever they can to make sure that those insecurities get bigger and bigger, and more and more sensitive so that you are easier and easier for them to manipulate and control.

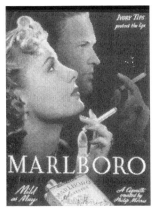

48

In the early 1950s the Philip Morris tobacco company said its Marlboro cigarettes were "Mild as May" because they were filtered. But Marlboros didn't sell very well because filtered cigarettes were considered feminine. So beginning in 1954, Marlboro ads promised men and boys they'd look real tough, like real cowboys—anything but mild—with a Marlboro. The Marlboro Man disappeared from U.S. media in 1999, but it remains a classic case of media manipulation of male insecurities. It's Exhibit A in the big, phony advertising, marketing and branding game that you don't have to play. What brands are trying to pull the same trick on you today?

Advertisers, in short, will not be happy about a Rebellion that helps you free yourself from your tight little male box and your young male insecurities.

And since television, radio and magazines rely on selling commercial time and space to advertisers, you can bet that large parts of the media will do what they can to defeat the Blue Sky Rebellion. At first they will ignore it. If that doesn't work, if the Blue Sky Rebellion starts getting traction, they'll ridicule it and try to keep you from participating.

Anticipating the Opposition's Attacks

The opposition's attacks won't usually be physical, using weapons and fists; mostly they'll attack with psychological, emotional weapons. Often with bitter and derisive laughter, they'll try to manipulate and control you with one of the emotions that most boys find terribly paralyzing: Shame.[49, 50]

They'll say you're being selfish. They'll say you must hate females. They'll call you a Neanderthal. They'll subtly suggest or tell you outright that you're a wimp, a weirdo, a loser, a jerk, a whiner, a fool, a troublemaker, a malcontent, a misfit, a freak. They'll say you're a disgrace. They'll say you disgust them. Shame on you!

They'll wonder out loud why you don't want to do what's "normal." They'll be angry (AKA frightened without being able to admit it) that you aren't going to do your "duty" and fulfill your "responsibilities" as a male.

And when none of that works, they'll drop the Atom Bomb. They'll call you a "faggot." They'll say you must be gay.

Self-defense for the Blue Sky Rebellion, therefore, consists mainly of Shame-Proofing.

Shame-Proofing

The possibilities for how people will try to shame you are endless, but you can learn how to protect yourself from the most common attacks. Keep in mind that not only will your opponents try to shame you personally, they'll also try to make you feel ashamed of all boys and men, and masculinity itself. They want you to distrust and keep your distance from your natural allies because "divide and conquer" is a tried-and-true tactic. So remember that the following discussion on shame-proofing applies to other boys and young men as well as yourself. Don't let the opposition make you think, "Well, I'm a good person. But they're right about how horrible other men and boys are."

Here are the attacks you can expect, followed by tactics you can use in response.

Attack #1: There's Something Wrong With You! Version A: You have a "Personal Problem."

If you're one of the very first to join the Blue Sky Rebellion, the opposition will try to make you feel that you have a "personal problem" by pointing around and saying, "Other young men aren't rebelling. What's the matter with you?"

Response to Attack #1

Remember the "Tale of One Island" earlier in this book? Remember the young Sea People on the island the evening before they crossed the mountains? At first they spoke in a sort of code only to their most trusted friends. Then they found that other young Sea People were thinking the same things. They built a team, they supported each other. They had proof they didn't just have a "personal problem."

If you join the Blue Sky Rebellion, it would be nice to have your friends join, too, wouldn't it? Maybe the best way to see if they're ready, willing and able is to ask if they've read this book or heard about it. Lend them your copy or tell them where to find it in the library.

An even easier and quicker way to gauge their interest would be to ask them to look at the brief video excerpts of President Obama at blueskyrebellion.com.

You might find that, like the young Sea People who were secretly growing plants on the island, your friends have been thinking and feeling the same things as you.

Another way might be to open a conversation with your friends about how boys are treated. If you see or hear of something at school, for instance, that you think was unfair to a particular boy or to boys in general, you can ask your friends what they think of that. Other possible conversation-starters are sitcoms and commercials that make men and boys look stupid, movies that try to get laughs by showing boys getting kicked in the groin, or news stories that lament the fact that "women and children" were killed without much attention to victims who happened to be men, the class of person you will soon be.

Also, keep an eye out for whether your friends avoid doing things they want to do because somebody might call them "gay" or do things they don't really want to do because those things are regarded as "manly." If you see a friend do something like that, just ask how he made his decision and if it was the decision he *really* wanted to make.

Until you find your allies you can say, "No, I don't have more personal problems than other boys and young men. Maybe what I have is just a little more information." Be confident while you're working to identify your allies that you are *not* the only young man who feels this way.

Attack #2: You're whining! Everybody's a victim these days!

It's very unmanly—and shameful—to whine, of course, so this can be an effective tactic if you're not ready for it.

Response to Attack #2

Here's what you can say:
"There's actually a big difference between a whine and a rebellion. Whiners just mope and complain, expecting somebody else to fix their problem. Rebels take their own action to fix their own problems. And they muster the allies they need to fix the problems that are too big for them to fix by themselves."

Attack #3: Boys and men already run the world! Just look at how much less money girls and women make! What do you have to complain about?

The opposition will tell you that "the real problem" (as if there is only one real problem) is that "women earn 74 (or 59 or 83, depending on who's talking) cents for every dollar men earn." They will say that before boys and men can have equal access to the domains reserved for girls and women, women have to earn as much money as men, women have to run as many big companies as men and women have to be half of all legislators.

They will say there is no way men and boys should have more options because we already rule the world.

Response to Attack #3

Most men do not "rule the world." More men are running around in pickup trucks with ladders and toolboxes trying to scratch out a living for themselves and their families than are sitting at the tops of big corporations.

There is no denying that before the modern women's movement women were indeed often paid less than men for the same work. But that problem has largely been eliminated. Today the number one reason men earn more money than women is that we have to. It is the main thing we're supposed to focus on. Remember the connection between expectations and obligations, and the difference between obligations and opportunities.

When you and your male friends are just as free as girls to choose your career because you love it, not just because it "pays well," when you can turn down a high-paying job because it requires you to commute too far and be away from your family too long, when everyone agrees that earning money is not your duty any more than it is the responsibility of your wife or girlfriend, then the Wage Gap will close. It can't happen any other way.[51, 52, 53, 54, 55, 56, 57]

A study of 22,000 adults in Finland found that men were less satisfied than women overall…"It is not enough for a human being to earn money and be in physically good condition. One should respect mental health as well," [the researcher] said.

ReutersHealth, December 5, 2000

You might have heard about the Lilly Ledbetter Fair Pay Act (the very first law President Obama signed when he took office in 2009). The law is a good idea because it gives people time to file lawsuits after they learn they've been discriminated against, but the popular story that Ms. Ledbetter received less pay than her male colleagues simply because she is a woman is inaccurate.[58]

Before we leave the topic of fairness and equity in employment, it's interesting to note how much attention is paid to bogus claims that women earn "only a fraction of what men make" and how little is paid to the solid statistics about employment fatalities. You, young man, are nearly sixteen times as likely to be killed by a workplace accident as the young women who are complaining about how unfair the "male-dominated" world of work is to them.[59]

Attack #4: Males can't have full and free access to traditionally female territory because males have testosterone. That's the problem. Testosterone poisoning!

Testosterone is the hormone most identified with maleness. The notion that testosterone is a poison is very strong these days[60] and it says a lot about how our culture is feeling about men, boys, maleness and masculinity. In particular, when men are violent and aggressive, too many people want to point simplistically to testosterone as the entire cause, rather than looking at the big picture of what causes men and boys to be involved in violence.

Response to Attack #4

Contrary to the stereotype, violence is not the exclusive domain of men. A 1993 survey of Canadian high school girls told them to think of violence as broadly as they wished and then asked who were they most afraid of. By a wide majority, they answered, "Other girls."[61]

Moreover, studies of normal boys, delinquent boys and highly aggressive boys demonstrate no link at all between testosterone and aggressive behavior.[62] A 1996 study[63] at the University of Montreal found that thirteen-year-old boys who were most aggressive and least popular had lower levels of testosterone than the popular, genuinely tough, but not physically aggressive boys.

Could it be that testosterone makes boys and men feel confident, secure and therefore calm? Could it be that not feeling confident and secure is what causes men and boys to resort to violence?

> "Testosterone causes aggression: that is how this research is reported in the media...The reality is much more complicated...By concentrating on testosterone, the quintessential male hormone, those who most loudly trumpet its alleged causal role in aggression and dominance do so in support of an ideological position."
>
> *—psychiatrist Anthony Clare*[64]

Testosterone is nothing for you to be ashamed of. You might mention to people who talk about "testosterone poisoning" that thousands of years ago an equally biased idea held that insanity in women was caused by their wombs. In fact, that's where we get the word "hysteria"—from the Greek work for uterus.

Attack #5: If males are so wonderful, why is there so much date rape and domestic violence?

The opposition will tell you that the occurrence of date rape and domestic violence proves we need more, not fewer restrictions on males. The issues are cooked to provide you a heaping helping of shame.

Response to Attack #5

Male violence against females is, of course, wrong.

Female violence against males is also wrong and deserves much more attention that it gets.[65]

Blaming boys and giving girls a free ride only exacerbates bad feelings and unhealthy relating between the sexes.

On the subject of dating violence, according to the National Center for Victims of Crime, "Both males and females are victims, but boys and girls are abusive in different ways." Boys are less likely to use violence in dating situations, but when they do they are more likely than girls to cause injury. Girls are more likely than boys to yell, pinch, slap, scratch and kick.[66] And, contrary to common thinking, girls are nearly as likely as boys to coerce a partner into unwanted kissing, hugging, genital contact, and sexual intercourse.[67]

On domestic violence, research that looks beyond police reports and women's shelters seriously challenges the widely held beliefs that males more often than females are the perpetrators, that women are domestically violent only in self-defense, and that women can't do serious harm to men[68, 69, 70, 71, 72, 73]. Domestic violence by women is under-reported because men are often reluctant to mention it.[74] They're often ashamed of being beaten by a woman and afraid they're the ones who will be blamed and arrested.[75]

Many—certainly not all, but many—domestic violence activists try to suppress the evidence of female violence against males.[76, 77] They also vastly exaggerate the amount of domestic violence committed by men against women. You may have heard that "Domestic violence is the leading cause of injury to women."[78] That's not even close to being true, as this chart shows.

Leading Causes of Injury Among Women Ages 18 and Older, by Age, 2006

Source: Health Resources and Services Administration, Maternal and Child Health Bureau. Women's Health USA 2008. U.S. Department of Health and Human Services. 2008. Source document includes notation "All of the leading causes in 2006 were unintentional."

Why would people want to distort the truth about domestic violence? They do it to shame you and pass laws that keep you in "your place."[79]

"Public service" advertisements in Dallas, Texas, November 2008.

Don't accept the shame. Don't let them keep you from joining the Blue Sky Rebellion.

Attack #6: You're so angry!

The opposition will try to bait you, to set a trap. "You're so *angry*," they'll say, as if that ends the discussion, as if boys have absolutely nothing to be unhappy, sad or angry about.

Response to Attack #6

First of all, anger can be a very healthy emotion. The question is what are you angry about and what do you do with your anger.

Anger is the only emotion boys and men are "supposed" to feel. It's the only one that's considered "male."[80, 81] On the other hand, male anger is treated much more harshly than female anger, so feeling justifiably angry can be tricky for us. A good way to deal with your anger is to dig deep into what you're feeling and to express the emotions you felt first—before you felt angry. [82]

You can avoid the Anger Trap by saying something like this. "I feel strong emotions, yes. But I only get angry—justifiably so—when people don't care about my other emotions. Mostly what I feel is sad and disappointed. I'm ready to talk calmly and openly about what I'm feeling. Are you ready to listen in the same way?"

Or you can say, "That's funny. I don't feel angry. I feel sad and disappointed. Maybe you're doing what the psychologists call projecting. Maybe you're projecting your anger onto me because you're angry about what I'm saying and you don't want to admit it."

Attack #7: Males aren't gentle, patient or nurturing. They aren't as good as mothers at taking care of kids. You can help women with parenting but you can't expect to be equal.

You might hear that babies and children need their mothers more than their fathers. You might hear about the "Nurturing Instinct" that only women supposedly have. You might hear that we males have no natural inclination toward helping children grow strong and healthy and so it is just plain wrong for you to insist on equal access to the responsibilities and rewards of parenting when you grow up. It's also possible that your own experience with your own father leads you to believe these assertions about fathers are generally true.

Response to Attack #7:

In the old days, people who wanted to keep women out of high-paying jobs talked a lot about a "Business Instinct" that only men supposedly had. They claimed all kinds of ideas that have been proven wrong: women can't lead, women can't make tough decisions, women don't want to compete, women can't do math, etc.

Today, people who want to keep males out of "high-loving" jobs as parents say that men have no "Nurturing Instinct." They assert that men aren't patient, aren't kind, are too rough, don't want to be with kids, etc.

Interestingly enough, kids get special benefits from fathers' typical style of nurturing—including rough-housing and firmly insisting that kids consider the consequences of their behavior on others. In fact, research clearly shows that children raised by single fathers have more empathy for others and are less aggressive (though not less assertive) than children raised by single mothers.[83]

Sure, there are many fathers who are not as nurturing as we would like them to be. But before the women's movement took place and changed the ways we think of what women "ought" to be, there were many women who weren't as good at science, math, business and government as they are today. One of the best ways to help and encourage fathers to be better parents is to make sure fathers know their fatherly capacity for nurturance is fully appreciated and respected.

And sure, there are many men who don't want to make parenting their full-time jobs. And there are many women who don't want to make business or government their full-time jobs. But both men and women should be free to choose the best combination of options for themselves and their families, without being saddled by sexist biases.

It is also important to remember that some mothers have a style that is very much like "fathering" and some fathers have a style that is very much like "mothering." Bottom line is that kids and families need all the healthy parenting they can get. The Blue Sky Rebellion insists that your ability to be a parent when you grow up is fully respected, encouraged and valued.

> "In the last 25 years, we've convinced ourselves and a majority of the country that women can do what men can do. Now we have to convince the majority of the country—and ourselves—that men can do what women can do."
>
> —*feminist leader Gloria Steinem*[84]

Attack #8: There's Something Wrong With You! Version B: You must be gay!

The opposition tries to make you feel that you have a very specific and shameful "personal problem" by saying, "You must be gay!" Someone might call you "a faggot" for daring to participate in the Blue Sky Rebellion.

Response to Attack #8

The fear of not being regarded as suitably "manly" is terribly frightening to many boys and men. It can be, in fact, an obsession. On July 18, 2009, a google search on the exact phrase "prove your masculinity" came up with 158,000 hits. When the search was switched to "prove your femininity" google found only 8,910 items. The phrase "man enough" was found in 930,000 places, while "woman enough" was in only 164,000.

If someone tries to attack you by saying "Blue Sky Rebellion? You must be gay!" you might smile and say, "Actually, since I joined the Blue Sky Rebellion I'm happier than ever being straight."

And imagine how good it would feel to say to a boy who belligerently asks if you're gay, "The only valid reason you could have for wanting to know whether I'm gay is if you want to fall in love with me. If you want to fall in love with me, say so, and then maybe I'll tell you whether I'm gay. Otherwise, I'll let you wonder because I don't really care whether you think I'm gay or not."

That would be pretty heroic.

A Man. Not a Man.

Justin took a final sip of coffee from his **cup** and smiled. He crushed his **cigarette** and then idly tapped his **fork** against his plate in a downtown coffee shop.

"Yep," he said to the young waitress. "When I threw that **pass** for the winning touchdown Friday night I yanked off my **helmet** and threw it thirty feet into the air. He tugged his **sleeve** to reveal his **wristwatch**. "Oh, well. Gotta go."

He stood, put on his **gloves** and took his **umbrella**. "So long," he said to the waitress as he stepped out into the freezing rain.

"So long. I hope you'll come back," the waitress smiled as Justin walked out the door. "Wow, he's cute!" she mumbled.

"Too bad for you he's gay," a busboy chimed in.

"Gay? What do you mean gay? He's not gay!"

"Hello? Are you kidding?" the busboy said. "Didn't you hear him? He said he wore a helmet and threw a forward pass. And did you somehow fail to notice that he was using a fork just now? He drank from a cup, smoked a cigarette, was wearing a wristwatch, his shirt had long sleeves, he was wearing gloves and he was carrying an umbrella!"

○ ○ ○

Every one of the things listed in boldface above was at one time "considered effeminate."

The forward pass was invented because the original running game of football, with its infamous flying wedge, was getting too rough and dangerous. The forward pass was intended to open up the game and make it safer. Some purists, though, derided it as "unmanly."[85] We can see remnants of that thinking even today in Australian Rules Football, in which "throwing the ball results in a free kick to the other team and taunts of 'Sheila! Sheila!' ('sissy! sissy!') from the crowd."[86]

When the helmet first showed up on football fields, Pudge Heffelfinger, Yale's three-time All-American from 1889 thru 1891 said, "None of that sissy stuff for me."[87]

In 1611 Thomas Coryat, an Englishman, saw table forks being used in Italy. When he brought them back to England, he was widely ridiculed for "feminine airs."[88]

Frederick William, an 18th-century Prussian king and father of Frederick the Great, beat his son for wearing gloves in cold weather because it was "an effeminate behavior, worthy only of Frenchmen."[89]

Wristwatches at first were considered effeminate because "real men" carried pocket watches. It was only when World War I fighter pilots found them handy that they became acceptable for "real men."[90]

Up through the Civil War, cigarettes were considered unmanly because "real men" smoked only pipes and cigars.[91] The derogatory term "fag" for homosexual male might be related to the fact that gay men were among the first to adopt cigarettes, which in Britain were and still are called "fags."

There were similarly arbitrary yet widely accepted reasons to conclude that cups[92], long sleeves[93] and umbrellas[94] were effeminate, too.

Perhaps this makes you wonder about other things you might be avoiding today only because some rumor, some book, some song, some TV show, some busybody, some uptight fool or insecure, miserable bully said they were effeminate.

"Considered Effeminate" would be a great name for a rock band.

○ ○ ○

That concludes our discussion of Self-defense, the tactics you can use when opponents try to shame you and keep you from participating in the Blue Sky Rebellion.

But let's be clear. The opposition will at times be fierce, strong and experienced. You will not successfully deal with every hostile encounter no matter how well-prepared you are to defend yourself. Courtroom lawyers have a saying about that. "There is the case you prepare to argue. Then there is the case you actually argue. And then there is the case you wish you had argued." You will feel that way sometimes ("I wish I had said…I should have said…") after opponents have tied you up with practiced rhetoric and bogus statistics. Even if you're ready to present your case and defend your cause, you can never tell how the argument is going to go.

Don't worry about it. The purpose of self-defense isn't to defeat your opponents, but to keep them from defeating you and getting you to give up the Blue Sky Rebellion. You might be glad to know that another Great American Rebel by the name of George Washington didn't win all his encounters with the opposition, either. In fact, some historians say that he lost more battles in the American Revolution than he won.[95]

But he was ultimately successful because he had important allies. He could not have prevailed in the decisive encounter over Cornwallis and the British Army at Yorktown without the French allies Lafayette and Rochambeau on his side.

Similarly, the Blue Sky Rebellion does not depend on defeating opponents; it depends on you persisting in the effort and winning allies. Right now, you have many more sworn enemies than friends, but the vast majority of people are in the middle, doing what they do and thinking what they think only because they've never heard or seriously considered anything different. They are all potential allies. We need to explain to them what we want and why, win them over, and enlist their help to make the Blue Sky Rebellion successful.

So now it's time for the two most important parts of this book, both about diplomacy, the art of building alliances.

Diplomatic Briefing

No doubt, there are allies, unknown to us now, waiting in surprising places for our call to action. Let's use that as our motivation to keep on plugging even when things are rough and it seems our opponents are all around.

First let's look a little deeper at the situation we're trying to change so we can discuss it with potential allies.

The Difference Between Sex and Gender

Sex is biological. Gender is cultural.

Sex refers to your body. Gender refers to the social characteristics that a culture applies to each sex. Sex/gender systems vary from culture to culture.

Perhaps the most famous illustrations of how different cultures can have different ideas of maleness and femaleness are anthropologist Margaret Mead's descriptions of three tribal societies on the island of New Guinea near Australia.[96]

Members of the first tribe believe that women cannot raise healthy children. They think that only fathers can help children grow up well, so they expect men to be caring, cooperative, gentle, nurturant, sharing, and concerned with the interests of others.

The second tribe leaves child rearing to the women, who force the kids to fend for themselves. Everyone is expected to be selfish and aggressive, and tenderness is taboo. There is not much gender difference between females and males, except that males are expected to do the fighting.

In the third tribe, the women earn the money and run the farming and fishing operations. They give the okay for weddings and other important village business. The men engage in the arts and spend a lot of time comparing their costumes and jewelry with each other.[97, 98]

So it makes you wonder: if we could tear down our sex/gender system and build a new one, what could we come up with? Do we still need to say "Men have to do this! Men can't do that!"? Girls and women have done a good job of changing how the sex/gender system treats them. The Blue Sky Rebellion can do the same for you.

Understanding the "Other" Culture and Understanding "Our Own"

The goal at the heart of the Blue Sky Rebellion is for boys and young men to have the same level of rights and freedoms that girls and young women have, while preserving and honoring all the good things about being male. In other words, we want what girls have: the right to be how we want to be and not be limited by narrow, sexist ideas of what was traditionally considered "appropriate" to each sex.

Generally speaking, males and females have different cultures, different customs, different ways of living in the world. Neither is better than the other. The Blue Sky Rebellion wants to make sure that boys and men have the freedom to pick and choose the things they like best from each. It also wants to make sure that all the good things about male culture are recognized and honored, instead of being demeaned, ridiculed and criticized as has frequently been the case over the past fifty years.

Take this brief True/False cultural quiz and then we'll talk some more.

1. T or F: Imagine a little kid coming up to you and saying, "I can't do it. Please do it for me." You say, "No, you can do it yourself. Try again and I'll be here to help if you need me." You are therefore less nurturing than a person who says, "Okay, since you can't do it for yourself, I'll do it for you."
2. T or F: Someone who gives flowers to a person is clearly more loving than someone who cuts the grass for that person.
3. T or F: If two people are talking face-to-face you can tell they are better friends than two people who are doing something together silently side-by-side.

A person who thinks "female culture" is superior to "male culture" would say each of these three statements is true. But encouraging a child to risk failure and accomplish something new can be a very potent form of nurturing—helping him develop confidence and independence. Doing work for someone can be at least as loving in its way as presenting a bouquet of flowers.[99] Working quietly with someone shoulder-to-shoulder can easily be as much an act of friendship as coming straight at him in conversation. All of those would be considered the "male" way of doing things.

So the answer to all three questions is False because neither approach is less or more or better or worse than the other.

A healthy person is able to appreciate both "male" and "female" styles of thinking, feeling and acting. It's like having two computer programs or operating systems on your hard drive, so you can call up the one you feel is best in any particular situation.[100] Rather than referring to the two cultures as "male" and "female" it might be better to refer to them as "Culture A" and "Culture 1." Neither is better than, more important than, prior to or above the other. They are both top-rate.

The fancy term for this flexibility is "androgyny" (pronounced ann DRAH jin ee; "andro" is Greek for male; "gyno" is Greek for female). Some people like to make fun of androgyny because they mistakenly think it is neither male nor female, when in fact it is the best of both—the ability to choose and access whichever one is preferable at any given time.

> "My 'kind, caring, sharing side' is my 'kind, caring, sharing side' not my 'female side'."
>
> —*writer Rich Zubaty*

It's also important to remember that there is as much difference *among males* and *among females* as there is *between males and females*. Males and females are much more alike than we are different. We overlap on the vast majority of things (we all eat, we all sleep, we all like to have fun, we all have hopes for the future). It is only at the extremes that the differences are really noticeable. A graph would look like something this, with more or less overlap depending on the characteristic or trait you're thinking about:

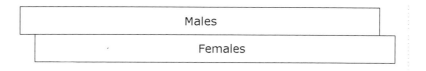

Appreciating the strengths of both Culture 1 and Culture A and letting you have the best of both is a major goal of the Blue Sky Rebellion.

Ready for Action

We've looked at our opponents and we've looked at the big picture we face. Now let's talk about the main work of the Rebellion: Making Allies.

Making Allies

This is the very most important part of the Blue Sky Rebellion. The world is a big place and we will need all the help we can get.

Here are a few general principles for being diplomatic and winning friends.

1. Remember: we are the Good Guys. If we can win our Rebellion, everyone will benefit. We have lots of love to go around. We're here to present solutions and work hard to make things better, not just complain about problems and throw a tantrum. *This is not the Department of Ain't It Awful.*

2. Often, the way you say something is at least as important as what you say. Female activists used to assert "For a girl to be seen as half as smart, she has be two times smarter." And so it is for us: "For a boy to be seen as half as loving or gentle or patient or caring or reasonable, he has to be two times more of all those things." That's not fair, but that's the way it is—at least until the Rebellion succeeds.[101]

Don't Shortchange Yourself

Imagine being shortchanged in a store. You know you should have gotten $15 change, but you only got $5. If you immediately become hostile and assume that the shopkeeper intentionally cheated you and accuse him loudly of bad behavior you're likely to meet with embarrassment, resistance, hostility and denial. You've become a problem and the shopkeeper will want to get rid of you as soon as possible. He might even call the police since he can expect them to take his side automatically.

But if you count your change and calmly say to the shopkeeper, "I'm sorry. I think you owe me another ten," and show him the hand into which he put your change, you're more likely to get a sincere apology and the money you are owed.

Now, certainly there are dishonest and selfish people in the world, and we will surely run into many of them during the Blue Sky Rebellion, but we're smart to assume first that people are honest and interested in being fair and to treat them otherwise only after they demonstrate that's what we have to do.

3. Always keep in mind why it's good, noble and heroic of you to be a member of the Blue Sky Rebellion: the world needs happy, healthy boys growing to be happy, healthy men, and the Blue Sky Rebellion can help the world have many more of them. Don't let anyone make you feel selfish for taking care of yourself and your young male friends.

4. When dealing with people who don't understand the Blue Sky Rebellion, stay calm and patient, and try not to let frustration get the best of you. A boy who is frustrated is almost as easy to dismiss as a boy who is operating from anger and forgetting his deeper feelings. Again, it's not fair, but according to the sexist biases we're working to overturn, a boy is supposed to be someone who is always in control—or at least pretends to be. Showing frustration gives people an excuse for turning away and ignoring you, like turning away from a politician who suddenly starts to stutter, a singer whose voice is cracking or a comedian who isn't being funny. And it encourages hecklers in the audience. If frustration is getting the better of you while you're talking with someone about the Blue Sky Rebellion, admit it before it grows: "I feel like I'm not going to be able to explain this to you, so I'm going to stop. I'll think about what you've said, you will please think about what I've said, and maybe we'll continue later."

A World of Possibilities

Now let's look at various types of people we want and need to have on our side, and how we might win them over. This discussion is by no means absolutely authoritative or complete. Diplomacy is more of an art than a science. If and when you come up with new or better ideas, please offer them to other rebels through the Blue Sky Rebellion website, blueskyrebellion.com. The website Forum is one tool that might serve well for that purpose.

Making an Ally of Yourself

You are your own most important ally in the Blue Sky Rebellion. For a time you might be your only ally.

Certain forces at work in the world want to break up that alliance, to make you distrust yourself. They know that if they can create insecurities in you, they can control you and make you do what they want, to satisfy their needs and desires, not your own. As we've seen, advertisers can be in this group. Girls and women can want to control you; so can other boys and men. Anyone who wants you to behave in a certain way that is not truly your own has an interest in making you feel insecure about yourself and then manipulating your insecurities.

Keeping yourself as a trusted ally—an honest, reliable ally motivated by confidence and your ideas of what you want in life rather than by insecurities and emptiness—is the most difficult challenge of taking part in the Blue Sky Rebellion.

Can You Talk?

One of the very most important ways that society controls us is by making us unsure of ourselves. And it makes us unsure of ourselves by restricting our freedom to talk about what's really going on with us.

Wanting to talk about something doesn't always mean it's a "big deal" or you "can't handle it." It only means that something happened or is happening, it's on your mind and you think you'd like to take it out of its dark closet and put some sunshine on it. Hearing other people say, "Wow, that must have been awful" or "That must feel terrible" or "You must be really disappointed" can affirm you and assure you that you are perfectly normal for feeling the way you feel. One of the worst things about keeping something locked inside is that it allows you to get infected with the nagging doubt that what is wrong is all your fault—a "personal problem."[102]

Your feelings are like your eyes; they're important and sensitive. Would you ignore a speck of grit in your eye just because it's small, because "it's no big deal"?[103] Your feelings are the spark plugs of your personality. Don't ever let anyone or anything disconnect or re-wire them. Don't ever let anyone or anything steal your ignition key.

One of the best things that happens when you really accept your feelings and trust them is that they can give you a sense of direction. They help you know which way is up. They can help you see how to advance the Blue Sky Rebellion.

Whether you're talking with girls, women, other boys or men, you should expect and demand respect for yourself and your feelings.

If you feel you want or need some professional counseling, look into it. If you can't or don't want to talk with your parents about it, start with another trusted adult. A guidance counselor at school might be a good place to start. There is no shame in seeking a hand with the problems of being young and male, especially in a society that seems to provide so little help or understanding automatically. If you're embarrassed about asking for help, think of it as "coaching" or "stress management."

If you can recognize and take care of what you're really feeling, you will always be your own best ally.

Making an Ally of Your Future

The period of your life between 13 and 23 is not *the* game. It's spring training, maybe an exhibition game. One of the most painful clichés in modern life is the popular high school boy whose life peaks way too early, as King of the Senior Prom, leaving him with only a long, slow, pathetic, shallow decline to look forward to for the rest of his life.

Glory Days

I had a friend was a big baseball player
Back in high school
He could throw that speedball by you
Make you look like a fool boy
Saw him the other night at this roadside bar...
All he kept talking about was
Glory days

—lyrics by Bruce Springsteen

Although it might seem like tomorrow is the end of the world for you, the more important question isn't how cool or popular you are from 13 to 23, but rather how well you are preparing to be happy from 24 to 94. That's ten years compared with seventy. (Who cares about how happy you're going to be when you're 24? You when you're 23. And who cares about how happy you're going to be when you're 94? You when you're 93.)

"Everything in high school seems like the most important thing that's ever happened in your life. It's not. You'll get out of high school and you never see those people again. All the people who torment and press you won't make a difference in your life in the long haul."

—Mark Hoppus, bass guitar in the band Blink-182
MH-18 *magazine, Fall 2001*

And for that matter being in the Blue Sky Rebellion really can help you be happier from 13 to 23, especially if you can make lots of allies while still being true to yourself.

Making an Ally of Your Sex Drive

Your sexual urges are nothing to be ashamed of. You are not a "dog" or a "pig" for thinking about sex, especially when you see healthy young women with attractive bodies who are thinking a lot about being sexy. Nature *wants* you to have those thoughts. "Beautiful" when applied to a girl or woman is at least in part just another way of saying "probably healthy enough to have healthy babies."[104] So when you see a girl with "beauty," Nature does not want you to stop and think about it. Nonetheless, you need to resist being a slave to Mother Nature and falling for her tricks. She cares about making babies; she doesn't care about you or your future. She'll take a healthy baby over a teen boy any day.

On top of the biological impulse, there are powerful social and psychological forces pushing you toward sex. You have this nagging doubt about whether girls—especially pretty ones—find you attractive, about whether you're a "real man."[105] And all your buddies are "doing it"— or saying they are. So you might do just about anything to "get laid."

But getting laid can be much more trouble than it's worth. Aside from concerns about disease, pregnancy[106] and false allegations of force or other dishonor on your part[107], there is the fact that sex is something girls "give" and you are supposed to "get."[108] The price you pay in terms of your dignity and integrity can be way too high.

> "[An] aspect of sexual behavior that defined a man's masculinity [in ancient Rome] was how much sex he had. Oddly, the right amount was not what we would expect; it was not very much…A large sexual appetite, whether directed at men or women or both, was considered effeminate [because] it tokened a lack of self-control, an inability to dominate one-self…[Emperor] Claudius enjoys sex too much, becomes overly fond of his partners, and so gives them control over him."
>
> —*Professor Nigel Nicholson, Reed College*
> *Class notes: Gender Boundaries in Ancient Rome*

In 1972, a researcher interviewed 462 college students about their sex lives. Follow-up interviews in 1997 revealed that the men who had not pursued sex when they were young were significantly happier as adults than those who had "gotten" sex as often as they could.[109]

For all the mind and power games that girls and young women sometimes play around sex—both before and after the act—the truth is that

43

they like sex too. They're a little like Tom Sawyer convincing his gulli-ble friends that they should pay him for the honor and privilege of whitewashing Aunt Polly's fence. If you can ever say "no, thanks" to a girl or young woman who wants to have sex with you, you might find it a deeply, personally empowering experience.

Don't press. Sex will happen. Don't give your power away.

The message is not "Don't ever have sex." The message is "Don't ever let sex have you."[110]

Making Allies of Boys Who Are Friends

We talked about this earlier in the section on Attack #1: "You must have a 'Personal Problem'." Winning young male allies is going to be hugely important, so you might want to go back and read page 25 again.

If your friends are reluctant to talk or seem unsure of joining the Blue Sky Rebellion, don't be upset. Keep the door open and demonstrate by your actions that the Blue Sky Rebellion is a good and happy thing. Show your leadership by your example, and remember that the best kind of leadership is the kind that helps people feel motivated within themselves by their own choice, not pushed or pulled by somebody else. It's okay to have strong discussions, even passionate debate, but under no circumstances should you try to shame or otherwise manipulate a reluctant friend—or anyone—into joining the Blue Sky Rebellion. That would only be making matters worse. You want to be a leader, not a dictator, bully or manipulator. Boys and young men have too many of those in their lives already.

Making Allies of Boys Who Are Rivals

As Steve Biddulph says in *Raising Boys*, "The rule is put down some-one else before they put you down."[111]

Boys who subscribe to that rule are probably under a lot of stress. "Everybody thinks you've got it so easy when you're on top," one popu-lar boy told a psychologist, "but being on top just means you have to worry all the time about slipping or somebody gaining on you. All it takes is one mistake or a bad day, and all sorts of people are waiting to take you down."[112]

So if there are boys around who would love to score points by putting you down about the Blue Sky Rebellion, it's probably best not to try to win them over right away. They'll probably just take a shot at you.

But think about how you can eventually offer them a better way. They certainly don't want to be on bottom, but that doesn't mean they have to be on top. Help them picture themselves in a group of equal partners, each claiming his own space, his own way of being genuinely "cool." Offer them the idea that they can decide for themselves which way is up, and everyone might have a different, equally respectable idea. If you're happy and confident, other boys might feel that the Blue Sky Rebellion would be good for them, too.

Making Allies of Boys Who are "Losers"

Boys want to feel that they are part of a team. They want to be appreciated and accepted for having something valuable to contribute to the group. They want their skills and talents to be recognized and put to good use. That's why we all cheer stories about the outcast geeky kid who saves the day and solves the case because he knows some wacky piece of information or has some special skill from his nerdy hobby. We all feel nerdy in one way or another. Great leaders know how to make everyone feel included and valuable. It's up to you as a leader of the Blue Sky Rebellion to make sure everybody who has something to contribute is welcomed and valued, no matter how "uncool" he might be according to this week's definition of coolness. If you can help a "loser" feel like he's part of a winning team, you will have a loyal ally forever.

Making Allies of Boys Who are Bullies

Angry and overly aggressive boys often do not feel confident about themselves and their standing among their peers.[113] We witness their anger and insecurity in their bullying behavior.

Bullying is often a public performance. An expert who helped develop an anti-bullying program in Kansas said, "The whole drama is supported by the bystander...The theater can't take place if there's no audience."[114] Along the same lines, psychologists Kindlon & Thompson say "Just as one boy's careless taunt can inflict a lasting wound on another boy, so can even a few boys change the climate dramatically with their decision to resist joining in the teasing or to stand up for a boy under attack."[115] By peacefully resisting a bully, just a handful of Blue Sky Rebels can prevent a lot of pain and trouble down the road because people who are picked on often try to "even the score."[116]

You can expect bullies to say that the Blue Sky Rebellion isn't manly, isn't cool, doesn't fit in, isn't for winners, that it's stupid and it's gay. It will be hard, but maybe you can say, "Before we know who's a winner and who's a loser we need to take a good look at the game, what the goal is and how you score points. You might score more points than I do in your game, but your game isn't worth playing. It's not making you happy. Let's make up a new game that gives us points for things we really care about so we can all feel like winners."

> The job of a Warrior is not to fight. The job of a Warrior is to keep the peace.

Making Allies of Boys Who are Gay

Gay boys and young men already know what it is to rebel against rules and expectations that don't work for them. They'll welcome, admire and appreciate your courage and your efforts in the Blue Sky Rebellion. Together you're working to make sure that boys get to be who and how they really are. You are natural allies. You're both working to make sure that the word "faggot" and the epithet "you're gay!" lose their power to punish, shame and control. At first, gay boys might mistake your newfound confidence as just another brand of phony macho posturing. It might take them a while to understand that your strength is genuine and that it generates safety and good will for others. Once they're clear on that, no doubt they'll welcome the alliance.

Making an Ally of Your Father

It's possible that your father is already an ally. If he tells you things like, "Find something that you love to do and make that your career no matter how much money it pays," and "Real men don't worry about who thinks they're real men" then you are way ahead in the game. Ask him what he thinks of this book. He might be able to give you personal advice about how to make the Blue Sky Rebellion a happy and productive part of your life.

Most boys are probably not lucky enough to have a father like that. In the section about the *Parade* magazine survey (page 12), we noted that men seem to oppose the Blue Sky Rebellion's goal of equal options for boys much more than women do. Why would fathers be more opposed to the Blue Sky Rebellion than mothers are?

Most fathers want what is best for their sons. But that doesn't answer the question "What is best?" Maybe one reason fathers oppose giving their sons more options is that, much more than mothers, fathers know how rough the world can be on men and boys who are different. Maybe, in an act of love, your father is preparing you to accept and be successful in the standard male role.[117, 118]

It's certainly understandable if your father feels this way. It was the same forty-five years ago when mothers were afraid that their daughters wouldn't find "nice husbands" if they participated in "that women's liberation stuff" and didn't settle for being proper homemakers. Your father might be afraid that you'll never find a woman to marry you if you don't make being a "good provider" your main goal in life. He might be right and you have to be clear on taking that risk; we'll talk more about that in the section in making allies of girls and young women.

Another problem is that hearing about the Blue Sky Rebellion might make your father feel sad about his own life. He faithfully fulfilled the traditional duty of being a "good provider" at great emotional cost[119, 120, 121] and now you're effectively telling him he could have gotten more out of life.

> "I've sacrificed a lot of stuff for my family because I had to go to work. I missed a lot of stuff in my life. And this is what we get out of it right here. It really hurts. It really does hurt bad."
>
> —*A 55-year-old man who was on strike against a paper mill where he had worked for 25 years*[122]

So make sure your father knows you don't want to throw away what he's done for you. You want to build on it. If you say it like that, he might feel happy for you and proud of how he has given you chances that his Dad did not give him, or was not able to give him.

Tips for Reaching Your Father's Heart

To get your father to talk about his real self—not his workaday, productive, economic self—ask him questions about his life:
- Who was your best friend when you were a kid?
- What was Grandpa like as a father?
- Tell me about the neighborhood where you grew up. Could you ever take me there?
- When you were my age what did you want to grow up to be?

Rent and watch the movie *Glengarry Glen Ross* with him; it's R-rated for rough and crude language, but nothing you haven't heard a hundred times before. It's a truly horrifying depiction of the pressure men can feel to make money. Ask your father to talk about the financial pressure he has felt and the sacrifices he has had to make because of it.

Ask if it's okay with him that you hope to have a life with less pressure to make money and more expectation that you'll contribute to your family and community in other ways that are also important.

If that goes well, watch the movie *Billy Elliot* (also rated R for four-letter words) with your father. It's about an eleven-year-old boy who gives up boxing lessons to learn ballet. At first, his father is far from pleased, but later he supports his son's decision. You might not want to be a ballet dancer, but you want to know your Dad will support you in whatever you decide you really want to do. The movie will help you have that conversation.

Making an Ally of Your Mother

Your mother's support for the Blue Sky Rebellion can be especially important to your participation because it can help protect you from feelings of shame that other women and girls might use to try to paralyze you.

Your mother has at least three possible roles and identities in the Blue Sky Rebellion. One, she is your mother. Two, she is a woman and might be at least a part-time member of the Sisterhood that urges women to "stick together" in making sure women and girls get what they want, with little or no consideration of possible unfairness or injustice to men and boys. Three, she is a human with a deep impulse to protect her personal interests.

First, if she is like most mothers your mother wants what's best for you. As with your father, the problem is answering the question "What is best?" Talk with her about what you think the Rebellion can do for you. Ask her what kind of man she hopes you'll turn out to be. Ask her what kind of woman she hopes you'll marry. If you like her description and share her hopes, tell her how the Rebellion can help get you there.

If she says, "I want you to be a 'Good Provider' who makes lots of money to provide for my future daughter-in-law and grandchildren by working ninety hours a week and becoming a stranger to your wife and children and dying of a heart attack by the age of 45," you're probably not going to be able to make her an ally. But there isn't much chance she's going to say that. She's much more likely to say, "I want you to pursue your dreams and be happy and healthy with a strong relationship with someone who loves you for who you really are. And maybe you'll decide to have kids and they'll love you warmly and deeply, and you'll raise them to be happy and healthy because I know you'll be a wonderful father." You can help her see that's exactly the kind of health and happiness the Blue Sky Rebellion is all about.

Second, if your mother feels a strong relationship with The Sisterhood, if she blames maleness and masculinity for various hurts and disappointments she has felt in her life, she might think that males need less freedom, not more. In a reverse paraphrase of what Darth Vader told Luke Skywalker in *Star Wars*, you might need to say to your mother, "Mom, I love you. But I can tell you're angry and suspicious of me because I'm male and some males have hurt you. But I am not your father. I am not your husband. I am not any man you have ever known who has ever hurt or disappointed you. I want to be free to grow up in a way those other men couldn't and I think the Blue Sky Rebellion can help."

Third, your mother is a human being with wants and needs and insecurities. If she relies heavily on your father's income, it might make her feel guilty to hear you say you want more options in life than your father had. Or she might be afraid that the Blue Sky Rebellion will make your father want to get out of his yoke and leave her stranded. If that's the case, she might be very threatened by the Blue Sky Rebellion. But you might be able to convince her (and your father) that it could be worth having less money if it means she can have a better, more relaxed, less money-focused connection with her husband.

(If you and your mother are going to say that, you have to really mean it. Are you willing to tell your Dad that you don't really care about expensive clothes or fancy cars or big vacations or big houses? Are you willing to tell him that you are willing to work your own way through school and/or take student loans and/or go to a less expensive college? If you are, let him know that's how much you want him to be available to you, so he can be the father and husband his family wants and needs. If you don't really mean it, all you'll be doing is putting even more pressure on him: telling him he needs to be more emotionally available to his family but no less economically productive.)

Finally, while we're on the topic of mothers, whether you join the Blue Sky Rebellion or not you should never let anyone pressure you to "grow up" or "be a man" by breaking off a close and loving connection with your mother.[123, 124] If you and your mother have a healthy relationship it will expand and grow to let you have the freedom and independence you need as you grow to be a man. Only people who want men to be dry, brittle, cold and hard—a lousy definition of masculinity if ever there was one—think it's bad for a normal, healthy boy to drink in as much of a healthy mother's love as he wants.

Making Allies of Schools and Teachers

There are good schools and bad schools, good principals and bad principals, good teachers and bad teachers, right? And let's not forget the librarians and guidance counselors. There are plenty of good and not-so-good people in those fields, too. Let's be optimistic and talk about the good ones first.

Some educators will really like the idea of the Blue Sky Rebellion. After all, it's about helping boys and young men feel happier, more appreciated and more motivated to be who they really are and can be. Good educators are all about helping young people reach their best potential. And educators are increasingly aware of and concerned about the fact that boys are dropping out of school much more than girls are, that young men are going to college much less than young women are. Maybe they'll understand right off the bat how the Blue Sky Rebellion can help lessen those problems by making young men more optimistic about what the future can hold for them.

So if you're lucky, all you and a couple of your buddies might need to do is tell the adults at your school that you're interested in the Blue Sky Rebellion and ask if they will help. Maybe you lend your teacher a copy of this book and ask if it can be discussed in social studies, maybe you ask the librarian to get a copy for the school library, maybe you ask the principal to discuss the Blue Sky Rebellion at a teachers meeting, maybe you ask a guidance counselor to consider whether he or she counsels boys and girls, young men and young women in the same or different ways.

Urge your principal to have training sessions for teachers in which they hear from boy-friendly educators, psychologists and others who can help them consider and overcome possible prejudices and discrimination against boys. If the principal says there is no money to pay for such a person, say, "No problem. We found one who will be happy to do it for free." Or you might say, "No problem. We'll raise the money ourselves." You and your buddies can mow lawns, rake leaves, shovel snow, have a bake sale. Wouldn't *that* get some attention!

Since it's so important for boys' success in school that they are up to speed in reading, check your school library. Does it have the kinds of books that you and other young men like to read? Does it have enough Blue stuff, to go along with the Pink? Offer the librarian some suggestions for books that would get more boys interested in reading. Librarians love helping kids love books. (A librarian at an elementary school in Troy, Michigan got boys much more interested in reading when, with boys in mind, she started a special collection of books called "Boogers and Farts."[125]) Does your library have enough books about the kinds of stories many boys are likely to enjoy—noble quests, struggles and adventures, for instance?

Whatever you decide to do, do it respectfully. Present the Blue Sky Rebellion as a solution, not as a problem. Teachers, schools and principals already have enough problems. They won't welcome a new one. Be confident, calm and cooperative. Be helpful. We're the Good Guys. Remember that.

The unhappy reality, though, is that lots of educators will not want to hear about the Blue Sky Rebellion no matter how you present it.[126] Boys need special attention? Yeah, I've got some special attention for you! Only it's spelled slightly differently. Replace the "a-t" with "d-e"! Detention is the special attention you wild, unruly and disrespectful boys need![127]

What can you do if your teacher or your school isn't one of the boy-friendly ones we all want and hope for? Here are some ideas:

- If you have a teacher you think is unfair to boys, don't sit back and take it. (You know that girls wouldn't accept a teacher who was sexist toward them.) Talk with your friends and see if they agree. If they do, start taking careful notes about how the teacher shows that he or she is unfair to boys. Include details: when, where, who was there, who said and did what. Then when you've got your evidence, ask for a meeting with the principal, talk with your parents, bring it up to the PTA, write a letter to the school board, contact the education reporter at your local newspaper. If that doesn't get the attention you want, start demonstrating quietly, peacefully. You might wear blue armbands, for instance, when you're in that teacher's classroom. Have fun standing up for what you know is right.

- If your school has special programs to help girls in math and science (the subjects in which many girls struggle), make sure it also has special classes to help boys in reading and writing (the subjects in which many boys struggle[128]). If it doesn't, do what you did with the unfair teacher: gather your facts and then ask for a meeting with the principal, talk with your parents, bring it up to the PTA, write a letter to the school board, tell the newspaper you've got a hot story for them. Don't take no for an answer. If girls' deserve special help with math and science, boys deserve special help with reading and writing. There are no skills more vital to an effective education than being able to read and write with confidence.

One other thing. You might think school is irrelevant. "What good is it going to do me to learn geometry? I'm never going to use that! Nobody is ever going to ask me to prove that alternate interior angles of parallel lines are congruent!" True enough.

But suppose you're on a football team. Suppose the coach lays a bunch of tires on the ground in an alternating left-right pattern and then tells you to step through them, running as fast as you can. Are you going to say, "This is irrelevant! I'm never going to have to step through tires in a game!"? No, you're going to know it's a drill designed to build skills that you *will* need to use in a game. And so it is with lots of school work. Sometimes it's a drill to develop skills that you *will* need in real life. Concentration, memorization, critical thinking, analysis, logic, problem-solving, creativity, perseverance, meeting deadlines, performing under pressure. Think of your teachers and other school staff as coaches for your brain.

Making Allies of Sports Teams and Coaches

What's the best and most important thing about team sports? Is it to learn how to win? How to be a winner?

No, it's about learning how to live and how to be a human. You'll win some. You'll lose some. No doubt about that. The most important thing for you to learn is that you can screw up—and still be great. The other most important thing for you to learn is that you can be great—and still screw up. On a healthy team, the only kind you want to play on, your teammates and your coaches will respect you no matter what, as long as you're a member of the team, trying your best, working hard, improving in every way you can, paying attention, helping out the other players. On a healthy team, everyone acknowledges that he or she has screwed up and will screw up again. There's no need, no effort, no desire to hide that. And on a healthy team, when it has just now been your turn to screw up, nobody forgets that they had their turn a little while ago and they'll have another turn soon. They'll help you through it. They know you'll help them when they screw up. And on a healthy team, if you've just now made a great play you're happy about that and your teammates are happy too. And you can't wait to get happy about somebody else's great play that's coming up soon—especially when you help to make it possible.

A team's job isn't to be perfect. A team's job is to adapt and change and do everything it can to be as good as it can be in whatever circumstance it finds itself. Sometimes everything goes great. Sometimes everything goes against you. Doesn't make any difference. The team is still working together to be the best it can be. A healthy team is always being the best it can be.

And what is the most important thing about a coach?

Joe Ehrmann was one of the baddest, meanest, roughest defensive linemen in the National Football League. But his heart changed deeply when he lost his younger brother to cancer. Writer Jeffrey Marx spent a season with Joe and his best friend Biff, the head football coach at the prestigious Gilman high school in Baltimore. Marx describes what he calls "the signature exchange" of the Gilman team under Biff and Joe.

"What is our job as coaches?" Joe asks his players at each practice.[129]

"To love us," the boys yell back as one.

"And what is your job as teammates"?

"To love each other," Ehrmann's players know to reply.

Biff picks up the theme. "I don't care if you're big or small, huge muscles or no muscles, never even played football or star of the team—I don't care about any of that stuff. If you're here then you're one of us, and we love you. Simple as that."[130]

Imagine two athletic seasons. In one, the team wins all or nearly all its games, but the boys feel tense and stressed for months, and the feeling carries over even into their non-sports and post-season lives. In the other, the team doesn't win as many games, but the boys end the season feeling more confident with themselves, with the world, with their place in it and with their ability to deal with it. Which season is better? No contest, right? The "losing" season wins.

So when you are thinking of going out for a team, ask the coach some questions. If he comes back at you all hardnosed and tough, if he makes it clear he doesn't support any of "that Blue Sky Rebellion stuff," maybe he's not the kind of coach that you really want and need in your life. If you don't get a sense of joy from him, you might have better things to do than try to make him happy.

What If You Are Just No Good at Sports?

Not every boy needs to play sports at a high level. We're all good at different things.

And remember that every boy's body grows, develops, matures and strengthens at a different age. Not being big, strong and coordinated enough for the varsity now doesn't mean you won't ever be big, strong and coordinated. Stay interested and give your body a chance to catch up. Your physical prime isn't when you're 13, 15 or 18. It's in your 20s and 30s. Maybe you'll like sports more later on.

Sports can be fun at every level, so don't rule them out of your life just because you know you can't be a super-star. If you're a "nerd" in the chess club and if you have an interest or desire to play sports, ask the other members of your club to join you in a pickup game where the goal isn't so much to win, but just to have fun and see what it's like to try to catch and throw a ball, and to help each other get better. Go out with the intention of having fun—including being able to laugh at yourself and each other. If there's a really cool super-stud on the school team, ask him if he'll come and give you some pointers—just for fun! If he's really, truly cool, he'll have fun too. And maybe you can show him how to handle a knight on a chessboard in return. If the Blue Sky Rebellion is about anything, it's about helping you to be happier and have more good times in everything you do.

Making Allies of Men

All the reasons we discussed about why it might be hard for your father to support the Blue Sky Rebellion apply to other adult men. And then some.

People who have had rules harshly enforced against them are often among the most cruel enforcers of those same rules when they take positions of authority.[131] Maybe they want to get revenge for what happened to them. Men who feel they were harshly forced into the small Male Box when they were boys might want to make sure you get treated just the same. "If it was bad enough for us," they seem to believe, "it's bad enough for you."

Or maybe they want to believe that what happened to them was right and good, so they feel justified in forcing it on others.

For many men, being in control—or clinging to the illusion of control—is the very essence of being manly.[132] Men who pretend that they are in control are not going to support a Rebellion based on the idea that men and boys are often treated badly. Also, lots of adult men are exhausted, beaten, depressed. Their attitude toward life is pretty hopeless. "That's just the way life is," they'll say.

Finally, lots of adult men are just plain afraid of saying anything that women don't want to hear—and many women don't want to hear that males have problems too.

All these factors can leave you without the vigorous, truly powerful adult male protectors and advocates you need and deserve.[133] So the best we can hope about a great many adult men is that they might join the Blue Sky Rebellion later on, after you've gotten it rolling.

But there are signs that a growing minority of adult men are ready, willing and able to help you take action right now. Around age forty many men realize that their competitive striving for individual success has been hollow. They begin to realize that the most important and truly powerful things in life are relationships.[134] They might want to help make sure your life is better than theirs have been.

> "Midlife is when you reach the top of the ladder and find that it was against the wrong wall."
>
> —*Joseph Campbell*[135]

Many religious congregations have Brotherhoods, Men's Ministries, and communities of men that go by other names. Some are beginning to deal directly with sexism against men. For example, an organization called the Men of Reform Judaism has developed a special ceremony for Jewish men called the Men's Seder. During the ceremony the men are asked to think about two very Rebellious questions: 1) Why is it that because I am a man I have to be the bread winner? 2) Why was it so much easier making friends when I was growing up?[136]

So see if you can establish relationships with groups of adult men affiliated with men's ministries in churches, synagogues, temples and mosques. They often need speakers and they might get a kick out of having an energetic young man come to talk with them about the Blue Sky Rebellion and how they can support it.

Making Allies of Women

Some women, perhaps many women, already understand that fairness between the sexes has to be a two-way street.[137]

> "The dialogue has gone on too long in terms of women alone. Let men join women in the center of the second stage."
>
> *feminist leader Betty Friedan*[138]

> "I gradually began to notice that [men] were suffering, too. Just as the fantasy of no control was the enemy of my self-esteem, the fantasy of total control was the enemy of theirs."
>
> *feminist leader Gloria Steinem*[139]

Women like that will welcome the Blue Sky Rebellion. After all, many women wish they had the kind of male partners Blue Sky Rebels will grow up to be, men who are more flexible in their actions, thoughts and feelings. Men who are strong without being hard. And they want that kind of men for their daughters, nieces, friends and colleagues to be able to love, live and work with. Many of these women will realize that Blue Sky Rebels are good for the world. And many mothers of boys and young men will see the Rebellion as good for their sons.

Other women, however, are going to be like some men were in the 1960s. Men back then came up with lots of excuses for why things either weren't really unfair to women ("women have it easy") or were unfair because they needed to be ("women aren't as good as men"). Some women will say the same thing in the other direction ("men run the world" and "men aren't as loving and caring as women are"). Some of these women just don't like males at all and see males as the source of all evil in the world. Others are so wrapped up in their own experience as girls and women that they simply cannot acknowledge that boys and men deserve attention, too.

Alas, We'll Never Make Oprah's Book Club...

In the early 1980s, before she moved to Chicago and national prominence, Oprah Winfrey was the co-host of a local talk show in Baltimore. On one program she unwittingly proved with crystal clarity that sexism against males exists and deserves attention.

During an interview with Fred Hayward, director of Men's Rights, Inc., an organization concerned with sexism against men and boys, Oprah tried to induce her guest to concede that though male gender issues might make interesting conversation, they are insignificant compared to women's issues. Hayward, one of the nation's most insightful commentators on problems facing men and boys as a result of their sex, was not about to concede any such thing.

Oprah pressed her demand for the concession. Hayward responded with laser brilliance. "Oprah," he said, "proportional to the population, there are eight times as many Blacks in jail as Whites. What does that tell you?" As a Black woman proud of her race, Oprah had a quick response. She said it told her that Blacks live under more social and economic pressure than Whites. Hayward agreed wholeheartedly, then moved in to close his case. "And proportional to the population, there are twenty-four times as many men in jail as women.[140] What does that tell you?"

What it told Oprah was that Fred's point was inescapable. She crossed her arms, turned away from him and refused to continue the interview. The director cut to a commercial and the producer told Fred, "This isn't going the way we planned. You'll have to leave now." After the break, Oprah filled the rest of Fred's time with an impromptu cooking segment, arguably less socially significant in Oprah's mind even than men's issues.[141]

Most women, however, will be somewhere in the middle. We will need to make perfectly clear that our goal is equality, fairness and moving things forward for everyone, rather than going back to the old days. And remember: "For a boy to be seen as half as loving or gentle or patient or caring or reasonable, he has to be two times more of all those things."

Making Allies of Girls

There are two main types of alliances you might want to have with girls and young women. One is girls as "just friends" and the other is girls as in "girlfriends."

Girls as "Just Friends"

Ask your female friends if they'd like to play a game. In "Round One: 1960" the girl tells you something she wants to do or be. No matter what she says, you say she can't do or can't be that—because she's a girl and you're applying the rules that were in effect for girls in 1960. Act as if you really agree with those rules and explain the reasons for them, using your imagination if you have to. When it's clear to both of you that sexist restrictions against girls in 1960 were ridiculous, introduce "Round Two: Today." Tell your friend some things that you want to do or be but can't because you're a boy. Tell her she has to come up with reasons for the restrictions and explain them as seriously as possible...without laughing. The game might help her see that the Blue Sky Rebellion is a good idea and make her want to help. Having girls on our side will help us make friends with other girls and with boys who would join us except for being afraid of what girls might think.

Girls as "Girlfriends"

Truth be told, it will take a very special girl or young woman to be the girlfriend of a Blue Sky Rebel—at least at first. After all, she'll have to treat you fairly and respectfully, never trying to use her sexual or emotional power to control you, never trying to shame or manipulate you into doing something you really don't want to do, never feeling threatened or jealous of your loyal friendships with other young men, always respecting your integrity and never treating your private thoughts, feelings and actions as gossip material to be "shared" with her female friends.

> "Women invent rules, manipulate men to obey them, and in this way dominate men—but in no way apply the rules to themselves."
>
> —*Esther Vilar in her book* The Manipulated Man[142]

And when you start going on dates with just the two of you she'll be fair about who pays. This is important because you will be setting patterns for your adult life. The expectation that you are the one who should pull the cart and provide most of the money severely limits your options and choices to do other things that might make you happier. She'll be willing to treat you "equally equal"—as equal as she expects you to treat her.

So you can abandon the Blue Sky Rebellion to have a girlfriend who doesn't want to treat you fairly, or you can hold on until you find a girlfriend in whom you can have faith and confidence.

That's really not such a hard choice, is it? Not if you have integrity.

So how can we make allies of girls we want to be our girlfriends? By being the best boyfriend you can be, by demonstrating that a relationship based on fairness, partnership and respect is the best kind of relationship there is, by making it clear that girls can't have better, stronger, truer boyfriends than Blue Sky Rebels. Great girls and women will welcome that kind of truly equal relationship. After all, many women are coming to the harried realization that they can't "have it all" all by themselves. They need equal partners as much as we do.

○ ○ ○

One of the good things about facing a huge and pervasive problem is that you can find opportunities for improvement just about everywhere you look. And so it is with us. We have a virtually unlimited source of allies ready to be won. They are all around us. We see them every day.

Now we must go out and win them.

Let the Rebellion Begin

The Blue Sky Rebellion will not take place in this book. It will happen in the things you say and do in your life. It will occur in the success you and other rebels have in supporting each other and in your efforts to win allies.

This book has given some suggestions for what you can do and how you can do it. A few additional ideas follow. Ultimately, though, you will be much important to the Blue Sky Rebellion than this book and its suggestions are. You and other young readers are the ones who encounter the real-life situations that need to be addressed. It will be exciting to see what you do and how you do it.

As mentioned earlier, the Forum at blueskyrebellion.com might be a good resource for you and other Blue Sky Rebels to talk and read about what is working best to advance the Rebellion. The discussion will probably start very slowly, so don't be afraid to be one of the early leaders to get things going. If, after you've participated in the forum for a while, you would like to be one of the moderators to help keep the discussion constructive and healthy, and to help keep our opposition from diverting, distracting or undermining it, please drop me a line at jk@blueskyrebellion.com. We will keep the Forum a "safe space" for you to say what you want among people who will be respectful, supportive and cooperative. (Other internet pages and groups will be more open to whatever comes their way, good and bad, constructive or not.)

Who knows what the future will bring? Let's keep tabs on how we can creatively use new Internet services to help you coordinate with other rebels and win new allies. ˆ

Additional Ideas to Get You Started on the Blue Sky Rebellion

- Organize your Rebel friends to gather signatures and send a petition to President Obama asking him to create a high-level White House Council on Boys and Men, like the Cabinet-level council he established for women and girls in March 2009. His address is:

    The White House
    1600 Pennsylvania Avenue NW
    Washington DC 20500

    (Old-fashioned paper petitions are often more credible and impressive than online electronic petitions, but you might prefer one of the online petition sites because they let you reach lots of people quickly and easily.)

• Call talk shows about things you feel are unfair to boys and young men. Remember to be upbeat, calm, confident.

• Start your own Internet radio show about the Blue Sky Rebellion. Or contact a local broadcast station about starting a public affairs radio show on boys and young men. Program directors at radio stations are often looking for good programs to be aired on weekend mornings.

• If your school celebrates Women's History month (March), tell the principal you and your Rebel friends would like to organize a Boys' History event that highlights the difficulties boys face—such as the high rate of male suicide, being more likely than girls to get arrested because they feel a need to act tough and make money, getting harsher sentences than girls for the same offense, and being killed and injured in dangerous jobs. If you want to take an international view, you can present how boys in Mexico are being used as drug assassins because they are "disposable"[143] and how boys in Pakistan are being brainwashed by the Taliban to be suicide bombers[144].

• Use the "Gear" available at blueskyrebellion.com to silently let other Rebels know that you're an ally and to prompt potential allies to ask about what you're wearing so you can open a conversation about the Rebellion.

• If you're in a discussion about something that has hurt you emotionally, reach down deep and check what you're feeling. As long as you're being honest, you are never wrong when you start your statements with "I feel…" (Note: this does not apply to bogus feeling statements like, "I feel you are an idiot.")

• When you see a sign that says "Girls Rule," change it to "Girls Rude" (unless that would deface someone's valuable property, of course).

• If you hear a discussion of racial profiling surrounding the arrest, search or questioning of a minority male, ask "How do you know it was racial profiling rather than gender profiling? Was he stopped because he was a minority or because he was a male? Or was it both?"

- Wear pink—or any other colors you might like. We talked about how things that are now perfectly acceptable for males were at first ridiculed as feminine. Pink is the opposite. It is now thought to be feminine but it was originally considered masculine because of its close relationship with the "fiery, manly" color red.[145]

- Write poetry and song lyrics about what you're thinking and feeling about the Blue Sky Rebellion. Offer the words to a local band and see if they want to make a song with them.

- The boys who can most benefit from the Blue Sky Rebellion might be the ones who are still too young to read this book. If you have a younger brother, cousin or neighborhood kid who looks up to you, help him keep his Blue Sky, protect him from some of the ugly messages you might have heard about what it means to be a boy. Help him be who he really is, who he really wants to be. Help him claim all the happiness in the world.

- Set up a Twitter account about your adventures in the Blue Sky Rebellion. If you want to do that, please let me know by emailing me at jk@blueskyrebellion.com. I can help people find and follow you by listing you on the book's website.

- During elections when candidates are in public forums asking for votes, ask them what they're doing to improve the lives of boys and young men.

- Go online to the Foundation Center (foundationcenter.org) or ask a librarian to help you identify foundations that fund research and programs for girls and young women. See if they're doing equivalent programs to benefit you and your friends. If they are, give them a suggestion of a program you would like them to fund. If they're not, write to them and ask them to write back explaining why.

- Make money by babysitting. Be the best babysitter any parents ever had.

- Use the Blue Sky Rebellion in your school assignments: short story writing, history, political science, psychology, sociology, economics…It really relates to just about everything in Social Studies and the Liberal Arts. Take the opportunity to talk about it in class.

- Dance! And don't worry what you look like. Dance by yourself if that's what works out best; you don't need the company of a female to make it permissible for you to have fun on a dance floor. Dancing by yourself isn't dancing alone. It's more like dancing with everybody, preferably with other Blue Sky Rebels included.

- Think about the kind of work you'd like to do when you grow up, not just the kind that makes the most money.
  - The world could use more male social workers.
  - The world also needs more male teachers, especially in the early grades.

> "I think that as men [teaching young children] we are making a profound revolution. It's not like the Berlin Wall coming down and it's not like there will be big bands. Every time a child and an adult see you or me in a classroom spending time with a child they have to deal with their beliefs. Why is that man there?…What we do on a daily basis makes a difference in what children believe that men are allowed to do in their lives. It shows children that, yes, indeed, men do care for and about young children."
>
> *Bryan G. Nelson, MenTeach.org*

- If you're thinking of asking a young woman out on a date with just the two of you, demonstrate the dignity of knowing that you shouldn't pay for the privilege of being with her any more than she should pay for the pleasure of being with you. Avoid establishing the expectation that you will automatically be responsible to supply more money to the relationship—whether it's for one date or a life-long marriage— than she will. Say to her, "I'd like to go out with you, but I have an ethical dilemma and a matter of principle that I need your help with. I have a big problem with the old-fashioned and actually rather sexist idea that men should pay for dates when they ask a woman out. Do you have any thoughts about that?"
  - If she says, "I deserve to be treated like a princess," consider saying—and maybe actually say, "That's fine. I deserve to be treated like a prince. So if I pay for the date, can I expect you to come over and do my laundry?" (Is her expectation that you will pay for the date any less sexist than your suggestion that she should do your laundry?)

- If she says, "The person who does the asking should do the paying," ask her if she expects to pay for her female friends when she calls them up and says "Let's go out." She will almost certainly reply that she does not. "So I'm not persuaded," you can say, "that the person who does the asking should do the paying. What else can we come up with?"
- If she says, "That's very admirable of you to stand up for yourself like that. Let's flip a coin and see who pays for the date. Or should we each pay half?" you have good reason to believe you are attracted to a very cool young woman.

- If you're ever in an emergency evacuation and some unofficial, unauthorized person yells, "Women and children first," yell louder, "No! Parents with children first!" Otherwise fathers who are with their kids will face the terrible dilemma of separating from and further traumatizing their already-terrified children, or keeping them nearby but in continued danger.

- If there is a comedy club near you, ask about Open Mike nights, shows that give new comics the opportunity to try their material in front of real audiences. See if you can make people laugh about what it's really like to be a young man these days. (The idea is that if they can laugh at it, they have to see it and acknowledge it and they have less reason to be defensive about it.) Find out how long the Open Mike emcee wants your act to be (probably something like 5–7 minutes). Keep working the same material over and over week after week, getting the wording and the timing just right. Don't expect to be funny at first. It takes a lot of confidence to be alone on stage without making your audience feel nervous and sorry for you. Eventually, though, your confidence will grow and when you can project that confidence to your audience, they'll relax and start laughing the way you want them to. If you're doing okay the emcee will let you go longer and longer week to week, adding and polishing more and more material. If you can put together 45–60 minutes, who knows, you could take your show on the road. If you have friends who would like to go on stage with you, try developing sketches, little plays, about the crazy things that happen to you just because you're young men. Maybe try some satire about the idea that "it's a man's world," for instance.

- Some boys have great experiences at all-boy schools, in large part because there are no girls around to be compared to and boys feel free to be themselves.[146, 147] Even though there might be girls in your school, don't worry about looking stupid in front of them. Be who you are, how you are. Do what you want to do. Say what you want to say. Ask what you want to ask. Learn what you want to learn. Forget about looking cool or tough or sophisticated, even if other non-Rebel boys make it a chief concern of theirs.

- On page 55 we mentioned how you might get in touch with church-based Brotherhoods and Men's Ministries. Along the same lines you can give speeches about the Blue Sky Rebellion to local service clubs like the Rotary, Lions and Kiwanis Clubs. Contact the club's Program Committee chair. He or she is in charge of lining up speakers. Service clubs tend to be business-oriented so in your talk be sure to mention how the Blue Sky Rebellion can help improve education, reduce juvenile crime and violence, and save money on police and jails. That will help keep taxes down and make your town a better place to do business.

Ideas Especially for Rebels in College

- If Title IX (which is best known for requiring schools receiving federal funds to have proportional male-female participation in athletic programs) has had what you consider to be an unjustifiable effect on your college sports teams, organize a demonstration to call attention to current male-female proportions in campus departments that are predominantly female. Ask whether and how those programs are reaching out to males.[148]

- Especially if you are starting your freshman year, you may be required to attend a session on date rape and sexual coercion. It will almost certainly focus exclusively on male responsibility for problems between the sexes and will give very little attention to the ways in which female attitudes and behavior might be part of the problematic mix on campus. Such sessions can have the unfortunate effect of shaming and demoralizing you or filling you with a sense of resentment and injustice. Prepare to speak up at the session by going to your campus library and reading the studies referenced on page 29. Don't be surprised or deterred if the meeting facilitators to try to dismiss your comments as wrong and unacceptable.[149] You will very likely find that you have allies, young men—and some young women—who agree that women, too, would do well to examine their attitudes and behavior toward the other sex.

Conclusion

You Have the Power

In 1975, inmates in New York's Greenhaven State Prison were preparing to serve as counselors for young people in trouble with the law. They asked a local Quaker group to help them develop ideas that would be good for the young offenders. The result is a program called Alternatives to Violence Project (AVP), now offered in hundreds of institutions and communities across the nation and around the world.[150]

The fundamental principle of AVP is Transforming Power—the belief that every crisis, every confrontation, every conflict is a bundle of power that can explode violently, can persist like a black hole of unhappiness sucking up your time and energy, or can flash in a brilliant light of creativity and betterment.

AVP lists five elements of Transforming Power:
- Respect yourself.
- Care for others.
- Ask for a non-violent solution.
- Think before reacting.
- Expect the best.

In the context of the Blue Sky Rebellion, we might think of the five elements as:
- Accept no shame.
- Remember Principle Number One: the Blue Sky Rebellion will make the world better for everyone.
- Look for allies to win rather than opponents to defeat. And be patient with your opponents; many of them will eventually understand.
- Check and understand what you are feeling. If you feel angry remember to check the emotions you felt before the anger.
- Expect to find and win many allies. Expect equality to one day be equal.

Godspeed, Blue Sky Rebel. You have the power to change the world.

Endnotes

Note 1: On April 17, 2009, Herman "Skip" Mason, Jr., President of Alpha Phi Alpha, one of the oldest and largest African-American fraternities in the nation, wrote to President Obama to urge the creation of a White House Council on Men and Boys. "We are keenly aware of the challenges that face women and girls," Mr. Mason wrote. "However, we believe a focus must also be placed on men and boys...Boys are in far graver danger than at anytime." As this book is finalized in mid-August, 2009, there is no White House Council on Men and Boys, but there is hope.

Note 2: Judith Warner, "Dude, You've Got Problems," *New York Times* "Domestic Disturbances" blog, April 16, 2009. The sociologist is Barbara J. Risman at the University of Illinois at Chicago.

Note 3: Maureen Dowd, "It's Over, Lady!" *New York Times*, June 29, 2008. A video excerpt of Barack Obama's speech can be found at www.blueskyrebllion.com.

Note 4: Morrie Schwartz quoted by Mitch Albom, *Tuesdays with Morrie*. New York: Doubleday, 1997. p. 35.

Note 5: "It may seem that every boy wants to 'be like Mike' (Michael Jordan). But it isn't so. Boys want different and complicated and conflicting things. Some want to be like Will (Shakespeare); others yearn to be like Bill (Gates) or Al (Einstein); while still others want to be like Walt (Whitman)." Dan Kindlon and Michael Thompson. *Raising Cain: Protecting the Emotional Life of Boys*. New York: Ballantine. 1999, p. xii.

Note 6: See, for instance, TARGET—The Academy at Rutgers [University] for Girls in Engineering and Technology.

Note 7: John Condry and Sandra Condry. "Sex Differences: A Study of the Eye of the Beholder." *Child Development*, 1976, 47, 812-819.

Note 8: Dan Kindlon and Michael Thompson. *Raising Cain: Protecting the Emotional Life of Boys*. New York: Ballantine. 1999, p. 54.

Note 9: The proportion of women who attend four-year colleges first exceeded the male college attendance rate in 1991. The gender gap has been widening ever since. [Mark Mather and Dia Adams. "The Crossover in Female-Male College Enrollment Rates." Washington: Population Reference Bureau. February 2007.]

Note 10: The gender disparity exists among students enrolled at two-year colleges as well. In 2006, men were 41.4 percent of students attending community colleges; they earned only 38.4 percent of associate degrees. U.S. Department of Education. Digest of Education Statistics 2006. Washington, D.C.: National Center for Education Statistics (2007).

Note 11: Here are the numbers of degrees earned by women for every 100 degrees earned by men in the Class of 2009:
- Associate's degrees: 167.
- Bachelor's degrees: 142.
- Master's degrees: 159.
- Professional degrees: 104.
- Doctoral degrees: 107.
- Degrees at all levels: 148.

(National Center for Education Statistics, Institute of Education Sciences, U.S. Department of Education, Table 258. Degrees conferred by degree-granting institutions, by level of degree and sex of student: Selected years, 1869-70 through 2016-17. Thanks to University of Michigan economist Mark Perry, Ph.D.)

Note 12: In 2007 in the U.S., about 632,000 juvenile females were arrested. The number of juvenile males arrested was 2.4 times as high: about 1,548,000. [U.S. Office of Juvenile Justice and Delinquency Prevention (OJJDP), "Juvenile Arrests 2007."]

It is sometimes noted that female juvenile delinquency is increasing faster than male juvenile delinquency. For instance, between 1985 and 2002 there was a 92 percent increase among females and only a 29 percent increase among males. But even at those rates, the raw number of female offenders increased by 202,500 while the raw number of male offenders increased by 267,100. [Juvenile Court Statistics 2001-2002. Stahl, A.L., Puzzanchera, C., Sladky, A., Finnegan, T.A., Tierney, N., Snyder, H.N. National Center for Juvenile Justice, Office of Juvenile Justice and Delinquency Prevention, U.S. Department of Justice Office of Justice Programs (December 2005)].

Some experts attribute the rise in the female rate to new zero-tolerance policies for minor offenses. If we look at violent crimes, the female proportion was only 17 percent in 1998 and was at the same proportion in 2007. It peaked at 19 percent in 2004. [OJJDP "Juvenile Arrests" publications for the years 1998 through 2007.]

Note 13: Males are 61 percent of U.S. dropouts between the ages of 16 and 24. The problem is especially severe for minority males. Between the ages of 20 and 24, nearly two in five Latino males and one in four African-American males are high school dropouts. "Left Behind in America: The Nation's Drop-out Crisis." Center for Labor Market Studies at Northeastern University, May 5, 2009.

Note 14: Friederike Range, Lisa Horn, Zsófia Viranyi, and Ludwig Huber. "The Absence of Reward Induces Inequity Aversion in Dogs." *Proceedings of the National Academy of Sciences*. PNAS Early edition. The research was also reported by National Public Radio, Morning Edition on December 9, 2008.

Note 15: Dan Kindlon and Michael Thompson. *Raising Cain: Protecting the Emotional Life of Boys*. New York: Ballantine. 1999. p. 222.

Note 16: U.S. Department of Health & Human Services, Administration on Children, Youth and Families. *Child Maltreatment 2006*. In 2006, the rate for boys under 18 killed by abuse or neglect was 2.5 per 100,000; for girls under 18, the rate was 1.7 per 100,000. For infants under one year of age, the male rate was 18.5; the female rate was 14.7.

Note 17: Article by Neely Tucker. p. C1. In the version published online December 30, 2000, the headline was "A Matter of Violent Death and Little Girls."

Note 18: Information for 2006 is from the National Center for Injury Prevention and Control, a branch of the U.S. Centers for Disease Control. Information for 1933 was provided via telephone by the Statistical Resources Branch of CDC's Division of Vital Statistics in March 1990 and is corroborated by Mortality Statistics 1933, U.S. Department of Commerce, Bureau of the Census. Government Printing Office, 1936.
In other countries, the male-female suicide ratio in the 15-19 age bracket:
- Australia (2006): 2.51. [Australian Bureau of Statistics. 3303.0 Causes of Death, Australia, 2006. Released March 14, 2008]
- Great Britain (2005): 3.22. [World Health Organization, Suicide rates (per 100,000), by Gender and Age, United Kingdom of Great Britain and Northern Ireland, 2005]
- New Zealand (2005): 3.1. [New Zealand Ministry of Health, Suicide Facts 2005–2006 data. Public Health Intelligence Monitoring Report No. 15]
- The male-female suicide ratio in the 15-24 age bracket in select OECD nations [World Health Organization data as reported by New Zealand Ministry of Health, Suicide Facts 2005–2006 data. Public Health Intelligence Monitoring Report No. 15]:
  • Canada (2002): 3.37
  • Finland (2004): 3.41
  • France (2003): 3.95
  • Germany (2004: 4.63

- Ireland (2005): 6.38
- Japan (2004): 2.07
- Netherlands (2004): 2.81
- Norway (2004): 2.78
- Sweden (2002): 3.67

Note 19: Yes, girls "attempt" suicide more often than boys do. But in August 1992 I interviewed David Clark, Ph.D., an expert in suicide and president of the American Association of Suicidology from April 1991 to April 1992. He said "the great bulk of female attempts are very ambivalent," meaning that many females who "attempted suicide" were not at all sure they wanted to die; many were trying to get help and attention for their problems. "Men, generally," Dr. Clark said, "don't attempt suicide unless they are completely devoid of hope." I told Dr. Clark that when I was an EMT on an ambulance in southern California in the late 1970s we had two back-to-back suicide calls. The first was at the home of a woman who had taken twelve aspirin and was on the phone crying to her girlfriend when we arrived. On the next call we had a man who had put a bullet through his head and was dead at the scene. Both would go on to be listed as "attempts" in the suicide statistics. Dr. Clark said those two examples were "good paradigms" of how males and females "attempt suicide" differently.

Note 20: Joan Ryan, "Sorting Out Puzzle of Male Suicide." *San Francisco Chronicle*, January 26, 2006. The director of the American Association of Suicidology is Alan L. Berman, Ph.D.

Note 21: NASW Annual Report – 2009. National Association of Social Workers, Washington DC. p. 16.

Note 22: This inability to see how sexism operates against young Black males is clearly demonstrated in a Family Therapy training video featuring renowned narrative therapist Stephen Madigan, Ph.D. The video shows a counseling session with a young Black male named Ollie who came to court-ordered therapy with his mother following an altercation at school. "No matter what color they were," Ollie's mother tells Madigan, "I never had no one to bother me, but it seems like once the boys get in that school district they really have to be careful. The girls can get out pretty good if they don't get to be bad girls, but the boys have to really watch their step real careful in every thing they do." How does Dr. Madigan respond? "So do you think," he asks, "that race had something to do with how Ollie was treated?" [Michael P. Nichols with Richard C. Schwartz. "VideoWorkshop for Family Therapy: Student Learning Guide with CD-ROM." Needham Heights, Massachusetts: Allyn & Bacon. 2005.]
On the ABC News program *This Week With George Stephanopoulos*, July 26, 2009, a few days after charges of racial profiling arose in the arrest of a black

Harvard professor by a white Cambridge, Massachusetts police officer, Donna Brazile, a black female Democratic strategist, said, "I'll never forget the lessons my parents would teach my brothers—not us [girls], but the boys" about being stopped by the police. Similarly, the Washington Post/Kaiser Family Foundation/Harvard University "African American Men Survey," published in June 2006, asked black men and black women if they had ever been unfairly stopped by police. Almost four times as many black men (48 percent) as black women (13 percent) answered Yes.

Research is needed to determine who is more likely to be stopped unfairly by police, a black teenage girl or a white teenage boy. Perhaps the wry term "driving while black" should be changed to reflect the dangers of "driving while male." Clearly the gravest dangers are faced by those who drive while black *and* male, but we do not yet know which is the greater risk factor. Maybe what we now call "racial profiling" would be more aptly termed "gender profiling." Though it does not address that question directly, a study in Massachusetts provides evidence that it would be worth pursuing. [Amy Farrell, Jack McDevitt, Lisa Bailey, Carsten Andresen and Erica Pierce. "Massachusetts Racial and Gender Profiling Study, Final Report." Northeastern University Institute on Race and Justice, 2004.] "Preliminary analysis from other jurisdictions indicates that young males may be disproportionately likely to be stopped, cited, and searched…Moreover, scholarship on profiling is only beginning to address the interactive effects of gender and race in an officer's decision to stop, cite, or search motorists." p. 5. "Overall we found that males were more likely to be cited than their representation in either the residential or the driving population estimate. Males were uniformly more likely to be subject to a search and to be cited than women." p. 24.

Note 23: Email from Sara Goodkind, Ph.D. of the University of Pittsburgh to the author, February 23, 2009.

Note 24: "Gender-specific services [are technically] defined as services that address the unique needs of the individual recipient's gender but [they] have largely been interpreted to mean services that are designed specifically for girls…Of course, boys have gender, too; however, this fact is often neglected." Sara Goodkind, "Gender-Specific Services in the Juvenile Justice System: A Critical Examination." *Affilia*, 20, 1. Spring 2005, p. 52 and p. 56.

Note 25: The literature on gender-specific programming for girls often comments that the juvenile justice system was designed "for boys." But the fact that it was designed to control boys and to protect society from boys should not be confused with being "for" boys in the sense of advocating for them or serving their needs.

Note 26: Will Glennon, author of *200 Ways to Raise a Girl's Self-Esteem*." In *Daughters* magazine, July 2001.

Note 27: Discouraging empathy in boys may contribute to bullying. See Winnie Hu, "Gossip Girls and Boys Get Lessons in Empathy." *New York Times*, April 4, 2009.

Note 28: See, for instance, Ashley Montagu, *Darwin: Competition & Cooperation*. New York: Henry Schuman. 1952.

Note 29: *Newsweek* touched upon the cooperation factor in an article about new research challenging widely accepted ideas from evolutionary psychology. Sharon Begley with Jeneen Interlandi, "Don't Blame the Caveman: Why Do We Rape, Kill and Sleep Around?" June 29, 2009, p. 52.

Note 30: On July 10, 2009 a friend who had read parts of this book sent me a link to a free, downloadable computer "wallpaper" image at truewhisper.com (a "resource for priceless words") showing a cartoon of a robust quarterhorse with a toothy grin. The caption says "The male is a domestic animal which, if treated with firmness and kindness, can be trained to do most things." The quote is attributed to British author Jilly Cooper.

Note 31: Terrence Real. *I Don't Want to Talk About It: Overcoming the Secret Legacy of Male Depression*. New York: Scribner. 1997, p. 77.

Note 32: Cathy Young. "The Mommy Tax: Is Motherhood a Boon or a Burden for Women Today?" *Reason* magazine, June 2001.

Note 33: In 1980, Report Number One of the NOW Project on Equal Education Rights (PEER) was sympathetic and insightful about the disadvantages of being male. It talked about how good it would be if "a man could quit a job he hated and take time off to retool, counting on his wife's salary to provide a psychic and financial safety net." As fair as it was, PEER apparently decided it didn't want to be *that* fair. In 1981, Report Number One was slightly revised and that male-friendly suggestion was deleted. [Project on Equal Education Rights, NOW Legal Defense and Education Fund. "Ties That Bind: The Price of Pursuing the Male Mystique."]

Note 34: See, for instance, Robin Leonard and Andrea D. Clements, "Parental Attitudes Toward Cross Gender Behavior." Document PS031066. Education Resources Information Center (ERIC). 2002. See also Coltrane, Scott. "Engendering Children" in *Childhood Socialization*, Gerald Handel (ed.). Piscataway NJ: Aldine Transaction, 2005. p. 302.

Note 35: Men: 25,864; Women: 23,218. American Bar Association, "Enrollment and Degrees Awarded, 1963-2008 Academic Years."

Note 36: See "More Parents Share the Workload When Mom Learns to Let Go," by Sharon Jayson in *USA Today*, May 4, 2009 for a popular-press account recognizing the problem of "maternal gatekeeping" and research into it. See also "Mother May I? Helping Moms Back Off So Dads Can Be Dads," by Sue Shellenbarger in *The Wall Street Journal*, June 17, 2009.

The National Fatherhood Initiative [www.fatherhood.org] offers a free three-session curriculum module called "Mom as Gateway" for mothers who would like to become aware of how and why they might unconsciously be erecting barriers between their husbands and their children. The module includes a four-panel Doonesbury cartoon that succinctly and deftly illustrates maternal gate-keeping.

In the first panel a father approaches a mother bathing their son. "Hi! Can I help?" he asks. "Help?" the mother replies. "No, you can't help."

In panel two the mother continues, "'Help' implies that caring for our child is basically my responsibility, and that you're doing me a favor. Go out and try again."

The third panel shows the father silently spinning on his heels and walking away.

In the final panel, the father returns and, as his wife directed, tries again. "Hi! Can I co-nurture?" he asks. "No," the mother says. "You always get the floor wet."

Note 37: The 2001 hearing was videotaped from a C-SPAN cablecast and transcribed by the author. The quote about the "proudest achievement" is from a White House press release, "Vice President Biden Announces Appointment of White House Advisor on Violence Against Women," June 26, 2009.

Note 38: In the mid-1990s a book called *The Rules: Time-tested Secrets for Capturing the Heart of Mr. Right* became a bestseller [Ellen Fein and Sherrie Schneider. New York: Warner Books, 1995]. It is essentially a book about imposing rules on men for the purpose of manipulating them into marriage. A few excerpts:

- "Don't meet him halfway or go Dutch on a date."
- "Invariably, we find that men who insist that their dates meet them halfway...turn out to be turds."
- "You will probably feel cruel when you do The Rules. You will think you are making men suffer, but in reality you are actually doing them a favor...They get to experience longing!"
- "[The woman] doesn't have to do anything more on the date than show up...don't make it easy for him...he has to do all the work."
- "It's nice of you to care about his finances, but remember he is deriving great pleasure from taking you out."
- "It's good when men get upset."

- "Let him be the one to worry about the future."

The book was so successful it spawned a series:

- *The Rules II* (1997)
- *The Rules Dating Journal* (1997)
- *The Complete Book of Rules* (2000)
- *The Rules for Marriage* (2002)
- *The Rules for Online Dating* (2002)
- *All the Rules* (2007)
- and a Kindle version of *All the Rules* in 2008.

The Rules inspired me to write a wry, pithy rejoinder, *If Men Have All the Power How Come Women Make the Rules?* in 1997. My agent in New York was sure she could sell it, but in the end she could not. One of the more telling rejection letters came from Rick Horgan, VP & Executive Editor of Warner Books, dated March 19, 1998: "While there's much truth at the heart of this, I didn't particularly like the one-liner approach, and the contempt this book would inspire among the women in house would be immense. I'll let one of my male competitors be the one who gets pummeled." This reply is doubly ironic. It unwittingly proved the premise of my unpublishable book's title, and it came from Warner Books, the very house that had published *The Rules*.

Note 39: As this book was nearing completion, I asked a friend to show his 18-year-old son the video excerpts of President Obama announcing the creation of the White House Council on Women and Girls and asserting that "women can do anything the boys can do—and do it better." (See blueskyrebellion.com.) My friend reports that his son looked at the video and responded that "discrimination toward women is far worse than discrimination toward males because there are so many more feminists." Without calling attention to his son's circular reasoning, my friend said he agreed there are many feminists and asked his son, "What do you think are some good examples of the discrimination?" but the son "couldn't come up with any."

Note 40: Peggy C. Giordano, Monica A. Longmore, and Wendy D. Manning. "Gender and the Meanings of Adolescent Romantic Relationships: A Focus on Boys." *American Sociological Review* (2006) 71:260-287. "These intriguing interaction results warrant additional scrutiny and exploration," the researchers noted, "as we did not have a theoretical basis for expecting these patterns." Perhaps, then, our whole paradigm of understanding the balance of power between the sexes needs to be rethought. See also Lev Grossman, "The Secret Love Lives of Teenage Boys." *Time Magazine*, August 27, 2006.

Note 41: William Pollack. *Real Boys: Rescuing Our Sons from the Myths of Boyhood.* New York: Henry Holt. 1998. p. 59.

Note 42: Anthropologist Margaret Mead, quoted in Marshall H. Klaus and John H. Kennell, *Maternal-Infant Bonding: The Impact of Early Separation or Loss on Family Development* by. St. Louis: Moseby Press. 1976.

Note 43: "Being a male is particularly hazardous during boyhood, when supposedly the male is culturally privileged by having greater opportunities for exploration and pleasure. [But] the cultural pressures on the boy to behave in traditionally masculine ways is much greater than the pressures on the girl to behave in traditionally female ways…[I]t is obvious that the 'blessings' of being a young male in our culture are extremely mixed. From early boyhood on, his emotions are suppressed by others and therefore repressed by himself. In countless ways he is constantly being conditioned not to express his feelings and needs openly. Though he too has needs for dependency, he learns that it is unmasculine to act in a dependent way. It is also unmasculine to be frightened ('scared'), to want to be held, stroked, and kissed, to cry, etc. While all of these expressions of self are acceptable in a girl they are incompatible with the boy's sought after image of being tough and in control." [Herb Goldberg. *The Hazards of Being Male: Surviving the Myth of Masculine Privilege.* New York: Signet. 1977. pp. 173-176.]

Note 44: "Girls and women…define what it means to be feminine…with positive language: to be compassionate, to be connected, to care about others. Boys and men…describe masculinity, predominantly…with double negatives. Boys and men did not talk about being strong so much as about not being weak. They do not list independence so much as not being dependent. They did not speak about being close to their fathers so much as about pulling away from their mothers. In short, being a man generally means not being a woman." [Terrence Real. *I Don't Want to Talk About It: Overcoming the Secret Legacy of Male Depression.* New York: Scribner. 1997. p. 130.]

Note 45: "Over the years, countless troubled [boys] have crossed into my office-slouching, 'underachieving' boys whose parents are at their wits' end. I often frame them in my mind as little protesters, sit-down strikers refusing to march off into the state of alienation we call manhood. If the choice is between success and connection, many boys simply refuse to play. We usually call these boys delinquents." [Terrence Real. *I Don't Want to Talk About It: Overcoming the Secret Legacy of Male Depression.* New York: Scribner. 1997, p. 188.]

Note 46: "We need to acknowledge that men are very afraid of each other at the deeper intimate level. This is an abiding culturally reinforced behaviour learnt at a very young age. There is a strong correlation between men's fear of intimacy with each other and their level of forced competitiveness." Kerry Richard Cronan, a psychologist in Queensland, Australia, in a posting to the listserv of the American Psychological Association's Society for the Psychological Study of Men and Masculinity, March 25, 2009. (Made public with permission.)

Note 47: Olivette Orme, "The Motherhood: An Unbreakable Union." *Wall Street Journal*, May 9, 1997. p. A-18.

Note 48: Thanks to Brian Sternthal, Kraft Professor of Marketing, Northwestern University.

Note 49: "Boys with a normal viewpoint were taken out of the fields and offices and factories and classrooms and put into the ranks. There they were remolded; they were made over; they were made to 'about face'; to regard murder as the order of the day. They were put shoulder to shoulder and, through mass psychology, they were entirely changed. We used them for a couple of years and trained them to think nothing at all of killing or of being killed. Then, suddenly, we discharged them and told them to make another 'about face'!...We didn't need them any more. So we scattered them about without any 'three-minute' or 'Liberty Loan' speeches or parades. Many, too many, of these fine young boys are eventually destroyed, mentally, because they could not make that final 'about face' alone...In the World War [World War I], we used propaganda to make the boys accept conscription. They were made to feel ashamed if they didn't join the army." [Excerpted from "War Is A Racket," a speech delivered in 1932 by Major General Smedley Butler, United States Marine Corps, Recipient of two Congressional Medals of Honor.]

Note 50: Roy U. Schenk was one of the first to recognize and analyze the impact of shame on male lives. *The Other Side of the Coin: Causes and Consequences of Men's Oppression.* Madison, Wisconsin: Bioenergetics Press. 1982. See also "Shame in Men's Lives." *In Breaking the Shackles: Bringing Joy into Our Lives.* Roy U. Schenk and John Everingham (Eds.), Madison, Wisconsin: MPC-BEP Press. 2002.

Note 51: Economist Nancy Pfotenhauer noted that women often choose to earn less than they could so they can take jobs that give them flexibility. "Women make decisions all the time based on things other than salary— enjoyment of the job and ability to have time with their families," she said. (Associated Press, April 3, 2001.)

Note 52:

Excerpts from an Interview about the Wage Gap
with Carol Iannone, Ph.D.,
vice-president of the National Association of Scholars,
an organization that combats political correctness in schools.
from *Good Will Toward Men*
by Jack Kammer

(St. Martin's Press, 1994)

Jack (speaking): Let's talk about the article you wrote about the case of Sears Roebuck versus the EEOC, the Equal Employment Opportunity Commission. The situation was that Sears was one of the most progressive corporations in trying to promote women through its ranks. Sears was making a good-faith effort to bring women into the corporation, give them good opportunities. Who was it who first alleged discrimination?

Dr. Iannone (speaking): It was the EEOC itself. Even though they compiled evidence for eleven years, they never found a single woman willing to say that she felt personally discriminated against.

Jack: So in the absence of seeing any real victims…

Dr. Iannone: They used the statistics.

Jack: They simply looked at the numbers.

Dr. Iannone: Right.

Jack: And the numbers were clear that women were earning less money…

Dr. Iannone: The big money is in commission sales. Very few women were in commission sales, selling the heavy-duty stuff: tires, furnaces, aluminum siding. You sell the heavy-duty stuff and you can make big money, but it's almost all commission. You don't have much of a salary. Plus, it's weekend work, it's night work; you go to people's homes, you work on a prospective sale for a period of time. That's where the money is. The noncommission sales are in the stores, selling bedding and pillows and things like that. You have a regular salary, regular hours, but you don't have an opportunity to make big money. And the EEOC found very few women in commission sales. They said this must be discrimination; women are not being allowed to take this better kind of work.

Jack: It's the patriarchy; it's men being threatened by women's success; it's male chauvinism; it's discrimination; it's an injustice to women.

Dr. Iannone: Right.

Jack: It's the Glass Ceiling.

Dr. Iannone: Right. Women are not being given these promotions, because somebody thinks they can't do it or shouldn't do it.

Jack: The idea that Sears was bad here is an idea that doesn't just reflect the EEOC's idea of Sears, but our society's understanding of our whole economy. If women aren't making big bucks, it's because of discrimination.

Dr. Iannone: Absolutely. If it isn't fifty-fifty, it must be discrimination…

Jack: Despite the best efforts of the EEOC to demonstrate discrimination, Sears demonstrated that there are other causes for what we popularly perceive to be a Glass Ceiling.

Dr. Iannone: Yes.

Jack: What are the other causes?

> *Dr. Iannone: A researcher, a feminist, named Rosalind Rosenberg, using the research that she and other feminists had developed, testified truthfully that women do traditionally take jobs that coordinate with family life, they do tend to like jobs where there is a regular salary and regular hours, they don't particularly like weekend and night work, they don't like the insecurity of commission sales where they don't know what they're going to be earning from week to week, they want a certain kind of flexibility on the job rather than having to give themselves over to it. All these things operated on women not wanting to go into commission sales…*

Jack: Was the EEOC believing that every woman was out there one hundred percent, working to try to make money?

> *Dr. Iannone: Yes. Or at least that was the tack they took.*

Jack: What happened to Rosalind Rosenberg?

> *Dr. Iannone: She's been vilified by the feminist academic community, and apparently booed at conferences; she had to take a lot of heat for telling the truth.*

Note 53: The National Committee for Pay Equity (NCPE) is a coalition of more than 180 labor unions, women's groups, and other organizations. It is largely responsible for the reports you keep hearing that "women make 59 cents [or 68 cents or 74 cents] on the dollar compared to what men make." This supposed "Pay Gap" is a misleading comparison. One reason for the inaccuracy is that fulltime working men work more hours on average than fulltime working women.

Some women insist upon a lesser focus on their paid jobs as their natural right. For instance, Laura Bellows, chair of the American Bar Association Commission on Women in the (Legal) Profession, wrote in *Ms. Magazine*, November 1995 "Why should commitment [to work] be demonstrated by working 100 hours per week? As women, we have other options to explore…"

For men, on the other hand, paid occupations are a major preoccupation. In an examination of 20 years of health and lifestyle data gathered on nearly 2,400 men and women, researchers found that unemployment, job insecurity and feelings of inadequacy in their jobs were all connected to at least a 50 per cent increased risk of high blood pressure in men, but not in women. "It may…be conjectured," a researcher said, "that the threat or reality of unemployment could be particularly devastating for men, for psychological and/or practical reasons." [Reuters Health; May 29, 2001.]

According to *The Australian*, April 11, 2001, "One female manager said that when she asked a room full of men who among them wanted her job, almost all put their hands up. The same question to a group of women drew only a few volunteers." The paper also reported that women "were more likely to trade off career development and higher pay in return for reduced hours and greater flexibility."

A prominent case of a woman having "better things to do" than take a job most men would kill for is the story of Abigail P. Johnson, a 39-year-old executive whose grandfather founded Fidelity Investments. As reported by the *New York Times*, Business Day section, May 22, 2001—the day after she accepted an offer to be a Fidelity division president—Johnson originally refused the position. "In 1998," the paper reported, "Ms. Johnson, now the mother of two pre-teenage daughters, said, 'I care about some balance and normalcy in my life.' Yesterday, however, she said she was ready to take one of the firm's highest profile roles."

When women have more options than men, when they feel free to avail themselves of more options than men, when they have more flexible and wide-ranging goals than men, we can expect them to be in more places than men. And since a person can't be in more than one place at a time, it is inevitable that women will be in fewer boardrooms. That is not men's fault. It is not something for which we need to feel guilty or ashamed. If anything, it is something we should demand for ourselves. Not only would that be good for us, but for women, too, because if men have more places they can be, there will be more available seats in boardrooms and management suites for people—men and women—who really want to be there.

Note 54: "Although additional research in this area is clearly needed, this study leads to the unambiguous conclusion that the differences in the compensation of men and women are the result of a multitude of factors and that the raw wage gap should not be used as the basis to justify corrective action. Indeed, there may be nothing to correct. The differences in raw wages may be almost entirely the result of the individual choices being made by both male and female workers." U.S. Department of Labor. January 12, 2009. Foreword to "An Analysis of the Reasons for the Disparity in Wages Between Men and Women."

Note 55: A study from the National Association of Social Workers is typical of allegations that male-female earnings differences result from gender bias. It observes that male full-time MSW-level social workers make substantially more than MSW-level females ($59,494 compared to $48,778). None-too-subtly suggesting the disparity is caused by gender inequities favoring males, the authors say the difference is not explained by reported years in practice. They do not mention whether the difference might be at least partially explained by other factors they noted elsewhere in their report, such as:

- Men are more likely than women to work full-time exclusively as social workers (80 percent of males, 73 percent of females).
- Women are twice as likely to be social workers only part-time (20 percent of females, 10 percent of males).
- On average, men work 8.4 percent more hours than do women (37.5 hours per week for men, 34.6 hours per week for women).
- A much smaller proportion of men (4 percent) than women (7 percent) work fewer than 15 hours per week.
- Women social workers left the field after a median length of 11 years while men stayed for a median duration of 25 years.

- Women are ten times more likely than men to switch jobs for more convenient hours (women: 10 percent; men: one percent).
- Eight percent of women left social work because the job location was inconvenient; no men reported leaving their jobs for that reason.

[Sandra McGinnis, Bonnie Primus Cohen, Paul Wing, Tracy Whitaker, and Toby Weismiller (2006). Licensed Social Workers in the United States 2004, Supplement. Center for Health Workforce Studies and NASW Center for Workforce Studies.]

Note 56: A study of lawyer salaries found no significant gender difference among lawyers who did not leave their jobs or work part-time to take care of children. It did, however, show a significant difference between lawyers who focused on their kids and lawyers who focused on their jobs. It had little to do with gender, except insofar as women are more likely to take the option of focusing on children. [Martha Neil, "What Gender Gap? Many Women Lawyers w/ Kids Do as Well as Men, Researcher Says." *ABA Journal*, May 12, 2009.]

Note 57: See Warren Farrell. *Why Men Earn More: The Startling Truth Behind the Pay Gap—and What Women Can Do About It.* New York: American Management Association/AMACOM, 2005.

Note 58: Karen Lee Torre, "Lilly Ledbetter Is No Victim." *Connecticut Law Tribune*, January 12, 2009. "Goodyear, like many employers, awarded salary increases based on annual performance reviews. Ledbetter's supervisor at the time of the alleged discrimination did not think much of her performance and she did not get a raise. Nor did Ledbetter get a raise in the last two years of her employment—for the same reasons of weak performance."

Note 59: U.S. Bureau of Labor Statistics. Census of Fatal Occupational Injuries, Table A-7. Fatal occupational injuries by worker characteristics and event or exposure, 2007.

Note 60: On July 18, 2009, a google search for the phrase "testosterone poisoning" generated 110,000 hits. The phrase "estrogen poisoning" produced only 15,700 hits. (Estrogen is the hormone most commonly identified with femaleness.)

Note 61: Patricia Pearson. *When She Was Bad: Violent Women and the Myth of Innocence.* New York: Viking. 1997.

Note 62: Anthony Clare, *On Men: Masculinity in Crisis.* New York: Vintage. 2001. p. 22.

Note 63: Benoist Schaal, Richard E. Tremblay, Robert Soussignan, Elizabeth J. Susman. "Male Testosterone Linked to High Social Dominance but

Low Physical Aggression in Early Adolescence." *Journal of the American Academy of Child and Adolescent Psychiatry*, Volume 35(10) October 1996. 1322-1330.

Note 64: Anthony Clare, *On Men: Masculinity in Crisis*. New York: Vintage. 2001. p. 35.

Note 65: "Screening for violence exposure should include both men and women...Further research on IPV among college men is needed." Elizabeth M. Saewyc, David Brown, MaryBeth Plane, Marlon P. Mundt, Larissa Zakletskaia, Jennifer Wiegel, Michael F. Fleming. "Gender Differences in Violence Exposure among University Students Attending Campus Health Clinics in the United States and Canada." *Journal of Adolescent Health* (in press). Published online June 1, 2009. The study found virtually equal proportions of university men and women reported being victims of violence in the preceding six months. Of those reporting emotional violence, more men (50.0 percent) than women (45.5 percent) said the violence came from an intimate partner. Of those reporting physical violence, nearly as many men (20.9 percent) as women (23.7 percent) said the violence came from an intimate partner.

Note 66: National Center for Victims of Crime. "Teen Tools: Help for Teenage Victims of Crime: Dating Violence." (Undated; accessed online June 27, 2009.)

Note 67: Susan M. Jackson, Fiona Cram and Fred W. Seymour, "Violence and Sexual Coercion in High School Students' Dating Relationships." *Journal of Family Violence*, Vol. 15, No. 1, 2000: 23-36.

Note 68: Murray Straus. "Future Research on Gender Symmetry in Physical Assaults on Partners." *Violence Against Women*, 12/11, November 2006. 1086-1097.

Note 69: Martin Fiebert. "References Examining Assaults by Women on Their Spouses and Male Partners" (annotated bibliography). February 2009. Department of Psychology, California State University – Long Beach. "This bibliography examines 247 scholarly investigations: 188 empirical studies and 59 reviews and/or analyses, which demonstrate that women are as physically aggressive, or more aggressive, than men in their relationships with their spouses or male partners. The aggregate sample size in the reviewed studies exceeds 240,200."

Note 70: BBC (British Broadcasting Corporation) "Newsbeat" February 10, 2009, reported that men in their early 20s are more likely than women of the same age to be abused by their partners according to British government figures. 6.4 percent of men in England and Wales between the ages of 20 and 24 say they were victims over the last year, compared with 5.4 percent of women. The definition of abuse includes non-physical forms like emotional bullying as well as severe force.

Note 71: "Whether we as a society are comfortable admitting it or not, many men are physically abused. Ironically, many of our assumptions, whether unspoken or otherwise, about battered men are similar to those we once held about battered women. 'Why don't you fight back? Why do you stay? You're so pathetic to put up with this.'" Linda G. Mills, J.D., Ph.D., *Violent Partners: A Breakthrough Plan for Ending the Cycle of Abuse.* New York: Basic Books. 2009. p. 35.

Note 72: "When it comes to domestic confrontation, women are more violent than men. The study...is based on an analysis of 34,000 men and women by a British academic. Women lash out more frequently than their husbands or boyfriends....'It's a complex argument but we do get more women aggressing against male partners than men against female partners,' [the researcher said]. 'The view is that women are acting in self-defence but that is not true— 50 per cent of those who initiate aggression are women.'" [*The Independent* (Britain) November 12, 2000]

Note 73: Contrary to common belief, women can do serious damage to men; some women are physically quite strong and powerful, not all men are physically strong and powerful, and women often use the tactical advantages of surprise and weaponry (including knives, guns and thrown objects) against men they intend to harm. It is true that injury serious enough to require medical attention is about four times as likely to result from a domestic assault on a woman as compared to a domestic assault on a man—one to three percent for female victims as compared to one-half percent for male victims. [Murray A. Straus, "The Controversy over Domestic Violence: A Methodological, Theoretical, and Sociology of Science Analysis" in X. B. Arriaga and S. Oskamp (eds.) *Violence in Intimate Relationships.* 1999. Thousand Oaks, CA: Sage. p. 23.] But there is no reason to believe this difference is a result of women's supposed moral superiority rather than mere physical disadvantage. And while most domestic violence injuries are not physically serious, they may be quite damaging emotionally and psychologically to men as well as women. Moreover, if twenty percent of seriously injured victims are male, we cannot rightly say that serious injuries to males are rare or insignificant.

Note 74: Public health researcher Robert J. Reid, MD, PhD said, "Domestic violence against men is under-studied and often hidden—much as it was in women 10 years ago...We want abused men to know they're not alone." [Rebecca Hughes, "Myth Debunked: Men Do Experience Domestic Violence." News Release. Group Health Cooperative Center for Health Studies. Seattle, May 19, 2008. Dr. Reid's full study: Robert J. Reid, Amy E. Bonomi, Frederick P. Rivara, Melissa L. Anderson, Paul A. Fishman, David S. Carrell, Robert

S. Thompson. "Intimate Partner Violence Among Men: Prevalence, Chronicity, and Health Effects." *American Journal of Preventive Medicine*, June 2008: 478-485.

Note 75: Denise A. Hines and Emily M. Douglas. "Men who Sustain Partner Violence and Seek Help: Their Abuse and Help-seeking Experiences and Implications for Prevention." Presentation to the 6th Annual Hawaii Conference on Preventing, Assessing & Treating Child, Adolescent & Adult Trauma. Honolulu, HI. March 2009.

Note 76:

> Excerpts from an Interview about Domestic Violence
> with Suzanne Steinmetz, Ph.D.,
> Chair of the Sociology Department
> and director of the Family Research Institute
> at Indiana University/Purdue University in Indianapolis.
> from *Good Will Toward Men*
> by Jack Kammer
> (St. Martin's Press, 1994)

Jack (speaking): Could you describe what you found in your dissertation data [in 1975]?

Dr. Steinmetz (speaking): In my dissertation as well as studies based on data collected from students in a number of countries, I looked at violence between husbands and wives, but I analyzed the data as couple data, without distinguishing who was violent, the husband or the wife. A number of colleagues asked, "How much of the couple violence is really husband-to-wife violence?" To my amazement, I discovered that the husband-to-wife and wife-to-husband violence were virtually equal.

Jack: When you discovered that, did you begin to doubt your research?

Dr. Steinmetz: No. I read the literature to see if there was anything that could account for what I had found. That's when I discovered that quite a lot had been written about the acceptability of women using violence on men. Historically, men who were abused by their wives were ridiculed as if there was something wrong with them because they could not protect themselves.

Battered men were publicly humiliated. For example, in France in the 1700s, they were blindfolded and made to ride a donkey backwards through the streets while holding the donkey's tail. They were made fools of because they had not lived up to expectations of masculinity.

Jack: Your findings must have upset the worldview held by a lot of people. Were you criticized for publishing your article on battered husbands?

Dr. Steinmetz: Yes. For instance, after the article was published, I was scheduled to give a speech sponsored by the American Civil Liberties Union in Richmond, Virginia. The woman in charge called to let me know that they had received

82

a bomb threat and that they were going to have police at the speech, but they didn't think anything would happen. And nothing did happen. Fortunately, it was all hot air. At the same time, I was getting calls at home from women saying, "If you don't stop talking about battered men, something's going to happen to your children and it won't be safe for you to go out."...I thought it was really ironic that they were threatening to use violence to stop me from speaking about women's potential to be violent. From their perspective, there was no such thing as a battered man— women just were not violent. Years after I had been promoted, I learned that this group of women had contacted female faculty at the university where I was employed and urged the women to work against me for promotion and tenure.

o o o

Jack: Why do nonviolent men stay in abusive relationships?

> *Dr. Steinmetz: Their reasons are similar to those given by women. They hope that the violence will subside. They are attached to their home, community and family. They believe that a two-parent home will be better and they are concerned that if they leave, the mother may become violent toward the children. Sometimes they do leave and then they try to fight for custody of their children.*

Jack: Do men sometimes stay because they're afraid they are not going to win custody of their children?

> *Dr. Steinmetz: Yes, definitely. No question about that.*

Jack: Could you describe the flaws that exist in surveys and studies using...police reports as their data bases?

> *Dr. Steinmetz: Because of the macho image, men tend not to report the incident unless they end up in the emergency room. But women, possibly because they hope that the police might prevent further violence, are more inclined to report lesser levels of violence. A woman who has a black eye suffers a lot of stigma and embarrassment when she reports that her husband did it, but there's even more embarrassment and stigma for the man who has to admit that the "little woman" did this to him.*

Note 77: Comments of Murray Straus, Ph.D., Director of the Family Research Laboratory at the University of New Hampshire on New Hampshire Public Radio August 15, 2002: "[The people with whom I was conducting domestic violence research] insisted on using a biased instrument. They refused to ask the questions about what the respondent did. This was for women respondents. They insisted on asking only the questions on what the respondent's partner did. That same procedure was carried over into the National Institute of Justice study, the National Violence Against Women study. They asked what they call a 'feminist' version of the Conflict Tactics Scale that asks only about victimization and leaves out the questions about perpetration. And, of course, if you do that you will have to find that only men are violent. And it was only after much pressure from people like myself that they then added a second sample of men. As a result, even though this study is biased in a number of ways—some of them unintentional, some of them intentional—they

83

found that forty percent of the past year assaults in this national sample of 16,000—which is huge and very dependable—forty percent were perpetrated by women."

Note 78: See, for instance, the American Institute on Domestic Violence <www.aidv-usa.com/statistics.htm>.

Note 79: There is also a lot of money to be made. According to Respecting Accuracy in Domestic Abuse Reporting (mediaradar.org) the domestic violence industry receives nearly $1 billion per year through three federal funding streams: VAWA (the Violence Against Women Act), VOCA (the Victims of Crime Act) and FVPSA (the Family Violence Prevention and Services Act).

Salaries paid to top staff at nonprofit organizations are reported to the IRS on Form 990. According to the 990 filed for the year 2007 by the House of Ruth, a domestic violence organization in my hometown of Baltimore, for instance, the executive director took a salary of $120,000, the Director of the Legal Clinic received $105,251 and the director of Finance & Administration got $107,532. Form 990 filings for many non-profit organizations are online at www.guidestar.org. Users need to register at GuideStar, but there is no cost for the service.

Money, of course, can be a corrupting influence. As *New York Times* reporter David Segal told Bob Garfield of NPR's "On the Media," on April 24, 2009 during a segment about media reliance on exterminators for data about insect infestations, "It's always tricky to get a sense of the scale of any problem from a party that has a financial interest if that problem gets worse." Similarly, H.L. Mencken cautioned, "Never argue with a man whose job depends on not being convinced." That wisdom applies also to women, of course.

Note 80: At a progressive seminar in Fort Worth, Texas for parents who are raising sons, the facilitator asked, "What's the only emotion that it's OK for boys to have?" The parents didn't answer right away, but after a few seconds they answered all at once: "anger." [*US News & World Report*, July 30, 2001.]

Note 81: Boy-friendly therapist and educator Michael Gurian writes, "By age nine, most boys have learned to repress all primary feelings except anger." [*The Wonder of Boys: What Parents, Mentors, and Educators Can Do to Shape Boys into Exceptional Men.* New York: Tarcher (1997) p. xviii.]

Note 82: "Anger is a normal human feeling, but it can be a tricky emotion for men. Psychologists call anger a secondary emotion, which means you simply don't get angry over nothing. Something has to hurt or frighten you first, and your anger is a reaction to your initial emotion. Some psychologists call anger the 'male emotional funnel system' because anger is one of the few emotions that society has permitted men to show openly. Men often convert other negative emotions (like fear, pain, loss, anxiety, or feeling vulnerable) into anger." Jean Bonhomme, MD, MPH in the brochure "Your Head: An Owner's Manual" published by the Men's Health Network, Washington DC, July 2008, p. 2.

Note 83: Warren Farrell, *Father and Child Reunion: How to Bring the Dads We Need to the Children We Love*. New York: Tarcher. 2001. p. 30.

Note 84: Gloria Steinem. "Revving Up For the Next 25 Years." *Ms. Magazine*, 8(2), 82-84. September/October 1997.

Note 85: "Football History Was Made Here at SLU," St. Louis University; "131 Years of Princeton Football," Princeton University.

Note 86: *The Complete Idiot's Guide to Aussie Rules Football.*

Note 87: Bruce K. Stewart. "American Football." *American History*, November 1995.

Note 88: California Academy of Sciences; Ludwig von Mises Institute.

Note 89: Mary Lou Derksen, "Childhoods of Famous People."

Note 90: Bob Brink. "The Art and History of Collectible Watches," *Palm Beach Illustrated Magazine*, May 2000; de Burton, Simon. "Tough, Rugged and Accurate." *The Financial Times*, June 08, 2007; The Timepiece Store, "The History of Wrist Watches," December 17, 2008.

Note 91: "Empires of Industry," The History Channel.

Note 92: Malcolm C. Grow. *Surgeon Grow: An American in the Russian Fighting*. New York: Frederick A. Stokes. 1918. p. 45.

Note 93: James Eason, University of Chicago class notes on Alexander Ross, *Arcana Microcosmi*, Book II, Chapter 16, pp. 179-184. London: Thomas Newcomb 1652. Eason discusses the Latin word *manuleatus* ("wearing love sleeves").

Note 94: "Ask the Globe," *The Boston Globe*, March 20, 1991. p. 82.

Note 95: The controversy surrounds questions of what is a battle rather than a siege, and what is a draw rather than a loss.

Note 96: Margaret Mead. *Sex and Temperament in Three Primitive Societies*. New York: Morrow. 1935.

Note 97: Luke Eric Lassiter. *Invitation to Anthropology*. Lanham, MD: AltaMira Press. 2006. See especially p. 127.

Note 98: Library of Congress (exhibit). "Margaret Mead: Human Nature and the Power of Culture."

Note 99: "Identifying love with expressing feelings is biased towards the way women prefer to behave in a love relationship." Francesca M. Cancian. *Love in America: Gender and Self-Development*. Cambridge University Press. 1987. p. 5. Dr. Cancian also says, "Both scholars and the general public continue to use a feminized definition of love." p. 71; "Part of the reason that men seem so much less loving than women is that men's behaviour is measured with a female ruler." p. 74.

Note 100: "I believe that when we can all speak a boy's nonverbal language of intimacy, he will feel more respected. When we can help a boy develop his verbal expressions of intimacy in a nonshaming culture, he will grow up healthier. When we can value action as much as talk, we will be stretching our gender values. When we can all hear and speak both languages, our relationships with each other will be richer and more satisfying." [William Pollack. *Real Boys: Rescuing Our Sons from the Myths of Boyhood*. New York: Henry Holt. 1998. p. 205].

Note 101: Meanwhile, the American Association of University Women, the group whose research purported to show that girls were shortchanged in schools, can issue intemperate and bellicose statements like this, and still be embraced by policy makers in the White House: "Because of our size, 100,000 members, we 'carry a big stick.' Because of our research, credibility is always a key part of our arsenal. Because of our history of achievement, we have a reputation for effectiveness. Because of our commitment to investing in our mission—'putting our money where our mouth is'—our adversaries know that AAUW is a force to be reckoned with, and that we have 'staying power' in our dedication to breaking through the barriers that we target. In announcing our new unifying focus, Breaking through Barriers, we are issuing fair warning—we ARE breaking through barriers. We mean it; we've done it before; and we are 'coming after them' again…and again and again, if we have to! All of us, all the time." ["Breaking through Barriers—AAUW's Unifying Focus." AAUW Current Topics Briefing #5; June 30, 2008.]

Note 102: "[I]f a boy gets to say, 'I'm hurt,' and he gets to say it over and over in an accepting environment, then he can recognize that he's hurt because it's been validated. If you feel hurt and nobody gives you the language and nobody validates the word, then after a while you don't recognize it as hurt. You recognize it as some kind of inchoate shame which makes you rageful." [Dan Kindlon and Michael Thompson. *Raising Cain: Protecting the Emotional Life of Boys*. New York: Ballantine. 1999, p. 292; (interview with Michael Thompson).]

Note 103: "If a boy believes that, in order to be manly, he must be 'on top' of his feelings, he lives in psychological conflict all the time because he's trying to control feelings that may be too powerful and complex to be controlled. When the conflict can no longer be suppressed, then depression becomes the psyche's way of surrendering." [Dan Kindlon and Michael Thompson. *Raising Cain: Protecting the Emotional Life of Boys*. New York: Ballantine. 1999. p. 159.]

Note 104: Your ideas of female beauty are by no means entirely biological. Just as advertisers want to install and manipulate your insecurities, they also glorify a manufactured and unrealistic ideal of female beauty so they can sell things—make-up, fashions, weight-loss products, etc.—to girls and women who feel pressured to measure up.

Note 105: "There is abundant evidence that sex was not as important, and certainly not as significant an ingredient of masculine self-evaluation, as it began to become after about 1780." Peter N. Stearns. *Be a Man!: Males in Modern Society*. Teaneck, NJ: Holmes & Meier Publishers. 1979. p. 59. It's interesting that 1780 was around the start of the Industrial Revolution, when many men's work moved from farms to factories, where perhaps they felt less like men and more like machines. Maybe men started using sex as a way to "prove" they were still men even though they now spent their days inside buildings "like women."

Note 106: Using a condom won't necessarily help you. Sometimes condoms break, of course, but you can be been forced to pay support even for a child purposely and deceptively conceived by a young woman who takes your sperm out of a used condom. Worse, the mother can with nearly total impunity prevent you from having a relationship with your child, leaving you with 18+ years of frustration and heartache—and very little help from the "patriarchal" system.

On April 29, 2009, a person using the screen name "nena14" posted this at askmehelpdesk.com: "can i get pregnant if i used the sperm of a condom? im really stupid i dont know what i was thinking, i lost my boyfriend 4 months ago but we still see and sometimes we have sex well when we had sex he left, so after 1 hour i saw the condom that we were using and the sperm was there so i open the condom again and i put it inside my vagina so am i pregnant?"

On June 6, 2009 a person using the screen name "Kira" posted this on Yahoo Answers: "Can the sperm in a condom impregnate me? I want a child. I am financially and emotionally stable enough to support a baby. I don't have a boyfriend, just a very good friend and we are sexually active with each other...I just want a kid as a single parent."

Note 107:

Excerpts from an Interview about False Allegations of Rape
with Rikki Klieman
defense attorney, former prosecutor and
adjunct professor of law at Boston University
from *Good Will Toward Men*
by Jack Kammer
(St. Martin's Press, 1994)

Rikki Klieman (speaking): I'll give you an example of a rape case I defended. A young man, a student at a college in Boston, goes out with a young woman, and eventually they go home together. He has roommates; they see this young man and young woman come in and go to his room. She brought her toothbrush, so she knew she was staying. Next day, she has breakfast with this young man and one of his roommates, and she goes off to school. About a week later he has not called her back. She asks him to a party. He doesn't want to see her again, for whatever reasons he has. He goes to the party with a different female, and the first young woman sees him there. Then she goes to a counselor at the university, and in her counseling session, talking about this young man, the conclusion is reached that he had sex with her against her will and that she was raped. The university police go and talk to this young man. He admits that he had sex with her. The next thing he knows, he is thrown in jail, a very bad jail. On her word alone. He has no idea what's happening.

Eventually I get the case. First of all, the university police knew nothing about any of the roommates having seen her the week before. They knew nothing about the toothbrush. They knew nothing about her having asked him to the party and his saying no. When I talked with young women in her dormitory, who knew her, she's described as being totally unstable. It wasn't like I had to do a lengthy investigation; they just handed this information to me. She's described as being a pathological liar by everyone, even her friends. In a system with a good prosecutor's office, when she first came to the police, an investigation should have followed.

Jack (speaking): Why did the investigation not follow?

I think it doesn't follow anymore because colleges and universities are afraid of being criticized. When they get a complaint like this, they just go for it. As I said, the pendulum has really swung. In many cases, young men are now the victims.

A more recent example of flimsy accusations of male sexual misconduct triggering nightmare scenarios for falsely accused males was the 2006 Duke Lacrosse Team travesty.

Note 108: "To be blunt, sex has historically been a commodity. It's a valuable source of power…Traditionally…[a] woman's most reliable currency was the potential of sex…Sexual power is…the female commodity." Carol Cassell.

Swept Away: Why Women Fear Their Own Sexuality. 1984. New York: Simon & Schuster. p. 31.

Note 109: ananova.com, July 3, 2001 and e-mail to the author from Whittier College professor Charles Hill, Boston Couples Study project director, July 13, 2001.

Note 110: So what are you supposed to do with all that reproductive energy Nature asks you to carry for it? Let me just point out that *Seventeen*, the popular magazine for teenage girls, said, "Polls suggest that a lot of people, both male and female, masturbate on a regular basis. So it's likely that some of your friends are doing it. But don't expect anyone to talk about it. When it comes to masturbation, mum's the word for most people." [July, 2001.] As of March 23, 2009, the *Seventeen* website says, "Masturbating is perfectly normal…As long as it's not excessive to the point of taking over your life and you aren't doing it because you feel like you have to, there is nothing unhealthy about masturbation." If a reasonable amount of masturbation (not doing it obsessively) is okay for girls, the ones who primarily control sex, maybe it's okay for you, too, no?

Note 111: Steve Biddulph. *Raising Boys: Why Boys Are Different, And How To Help Them Become Happy and Well-Balanced Men.* Lane Cove NSW Australia: Finch Publishing. 1998. p. 141.

Note 112: Dan Kindlon and Michael Thompson. *Raising Cain: Protecting the Emotional Life of Boys.* New York: Ballantine. 1999. p. 75.

Note 113: Dan Kindlon and Michael Thompson. *Raising Cain: Protecting the Emotional Life of Boys.* New York: Ballantine. 1999. p. 225.

Note 114: Nadya Labi, Rita Healy, Marc Hequet, Collette McKenna-Parker. "Let Bullies Beware." *Time* magazine, April 2, 2001, p. 47.

Note 115: Dan Kindlon and Michael Thompson. *Raising Cain: Protecting the Emotional Life of Boys.* New York: Ballantine. 1999. p. 76.

Note 116: "[In the fall of 2000] the National Threat Assessment Center, run by the U.S. Secret Service, found that in more than two-thirds of 37 recent school shootings, the attackers felt 'persecuted, bullied, threatened, attacked or injured.'" [Nadya Labi, Rita Healy, Marc Hequet, Collette McKenna-Parker. "Let Bullies Beware." *Time magazine*, April 2, 2001; p. 46.]

Note 117: "Given the 'beehive' nature of soccer at this age [five and six years old], most of the boys were in a pack, following the ball around wherever it went. Slower boys were not getting a chance to kick the ball. At one point, a young boy was about to kick the ball, then quickly stepped aside and said to a boy on the other team, 'You kick it, David. It's your turn!' His father was outraged. 'What are you doing?' he screamed from the bleachers. 'You're acting like a girl. You've got to be aggressive.' The boy immediately ran crying from the field toward his father. But his father turned him back toward the field, saying, 'Get back out there. You've got to fight for the ball.' In extreme cases like this one, the strict enforcement of traditional masculinity roles leads to a sense of abandonment, and tends to extinguish behavior that reaches toward emotional connection with a caregiver." John M. Robertson and David S. Shepard, "The Psychological Development of Boys" in *Counseling Troubled Boys: A Guidebook for Professionals*, Mark S. Kiselica, Matt Englar-Carlson and Arthur M. Horne (eds.). New York: Taylor & Francis Routledge, 2008.

Note 118: "The tragic bind for boys and men in traditional socialization is that in order to demonstrate themselves worthy of human connection they must perform competitively, they must become winners, which intrinsically demands disconnection, the exact opposite of what they truly seek." Terrence Real. *I Don't Want to Talk About It: Overcoming the Secret Legacy of Male Depression.* New York: Scribner. 1997. p. 178.

Note 119: "All the managers [fathers] interviewed were aware of times when they had been physically present but emotionally absent as a result of being pre-occupied with solving work-related problems...All managers expressed frustration over their difficulty in switching styles from their 'I'm the boss" role to 'I'm the father." T. DeLong and C.C. DeLong, "Managers as Fathers: Hope on the Homefront," *Human Resource Management* 31, Fall 1992: pp. 171-181.

Note 120: "Much of the work being done in the business bureaucracies was dull; it was hard to imagine oneself a bull male while pushing papers about a desk...Many white-collar workers fell back on their own version of instrumentalism, wrapping their manhood in their earning level and in the material symbols this could acquire. The jungle, the lair of the competitive hunting male, turned into the rat race, where the war was for survival and self-justification as a good provider. The goal was to prove one could hang on in a bureaucratic slot, where men easily exaggerated their struggles, and to prove to other men, and to one's woman, that one could hack out an improving standard of living. All of this could keep men slogging away at jobs that they could not even admit they did not like." [Peter N. Stearns. *Be a Man!: Males in Modern Society*. Teaneck, NJ: Holmes & Meier Publishers. 1979. pp. 149-150.]

Note 121: "Traditional work patterns lock women into second rate careers and lock men out of family life, risking damage to the mental health of both sexes. There's even more prejudice against men than there is against women if they attempt to build careers around family responsibilities." Carolyn Quadrio, M.D., psychiatrist and author of a 1996 study on part-time work. Australian Associated Press, April 17, 1996.

Note 122: NPR "All Things Considered," August 21, 2001.

Note 123: "There is no point—not at age four, or nine, or thirteen when a boy must 'give up' his mother, or when a mother must 'give up' her son." [Dan Kindlon and Michael Thompson. *Raising Cain: Protecting the Emotional Life of Boys*. New York: Ballantine. 1999. p. 116.]

Note 124: "Far from making a boy act in 'girl-like' ways, a loving mother actually plays an integral role in helping a boy develop his masculinity—the self-esteem and strength of character he needs to feel confident in his own masculine self." William Pollack. *Real Boys: Rescuing Our Sons from the Myths of Boyhood*. New York: Henry Holt. 1998. p. 81.

Note 125: Gina Damron, "To Get Boys to Read, Yuck Works Wonders." *Detroit Free Press*, January 25, 2007.

Note 126: Some influential education advocates care very little about boys. A 1991 report[126] from the American Association of University Women (AAUW) that alleged girls were being "shortchanged" in schools made national headlines. AAUW also discovered ways in which boys, too, were being shortchanged in schools, but they didn't publish that information.

Data gathered but not published by AAUW
as part of its 1990 Self-Esteem Survey

reported by Christina Hoff Sommers in her book
The War Against Boys[126]

*Note: these perceptions were registered in 1990,
before the current emphasis on girls' needs had even begun.*

Source: AAUW/Greenberg-Lake Full Data Report
Expectations and Aspirations: Gender Roles and Self-Esteem

	Girls %	Boys %
1. Who do teachers think are smarter?		
Teachers think boys are smarter	13	26
Teachers think girls are smarter	**81**	**69**
Other response	5	5
2. Whom do teachers punish more often?		
Teachers punish boys more often	**92**	**90**
Teachers punish girls more often	5	8
Other response	3	2

	Girls %	Boys %
3. Whom do teachers compliment more often?		
Teachers compliment boys more often	7	15
Teachers compliment girls more often	**89**	**81**
Other response	5	4
4. Whom do teachers like to be around?		
Teachers like to be around boys more	12	21
Teachers like to be around girls more	**80**	**73**
Other response	8	6
5. To whom do teachers pay more attention?		
Teachers pay more attention to boys	33	29
Teachers pay more attention to girls	**57**	**64**
Other response	10	7
6. Whom do teachers call on more often?		
Teachers call on boys more often	35	36
Teachers call on girls more often	**57**	**59**
Other response	8	5

After boys' educational difficulties gained attention of their own, AAUW issued another report in 2008 denying that boys as a class have problems in school.[126] The report reveals its ideological bias most clearly by asserting a misleading fact of little relevance to current educational outcomes as its most important proof: "Perhaps the most compelling evidence against the existence of a boys' crisis is that men continue to outearn women in the workplace."

Note 127: The Human Relations Advisory Committee of the school board in Fairfax, Virginia reports that it "received numerous comments that both boys and girls misbehave and disrupt classes in covert and overt ways as actors, manipulators, or instigators but that it tends to be the boys who are most often caught and punished…and that boys, particularly minority boys, are treated more harshly than girls in both the imposition of punishment and the severity of punishment. Finally, there are concerns that boys are perceived or assumed to have a propensity for misbehavior which results in disparate treatment and, over time, leads to a self-fulfilling prophecy." [Fairfax County (Virginia) School Board Human Relations Advisory Committee Annual Report, 2000–2001.]

William Pollack makes the same point in his book *Real Boys*. "Because the myth of boys' toxicity is still deeply entrenched within many school systems," he writes, "teachers and school administrators are often permitted to become hostile toward boys—and so they may push our sons even further toward academic failure, low self-esteem, conduct disorders, and a host of other emotional and behavioral problems." [*Real Boys: Rescuing Our Sons from the Myths of Boyhood.* New York: Henry Holt, 1998. p. 232.] Pollack has said "Schools—especially

big coed schools—are some of the most boy-unfriendly places in America."
[Cecilia Goodnow, "Author Warns of 'Crisis in Boyhood'." *Seattle Post-Intelligencer*. May 20, 1999. p. D1.

Note 128: Boys lag behind girls in reading and writing by two and three times as much as girls lag behind boys in math and science, yet there are few special programs to help boys in those crucial skills. Marjorie Coeyman. "Where the Gender Gap Gets Its Start." *Christian Science Monitor*. May 29, 2001. pg. 20.

Note 129: Joe Ehrmann has guidelines for great coaching at buildingmenandwomen.org.

Note 130: Jeffrey Marx. *Season of Life: A Football Star, a Boy, a Journey to Manhood*. New York: Simon & Schuster, 2003.

Note 131: "Those who have suffered society's intolerance can become equally hostile toward others' deviation from the norm." Aaron Kipnis. *Knights Without Armor: A Practical Guide for Men in Quest of Masculine Soul*. Los Angeles: Tarcher. 1991, p. 30. Kipnis refers specifically to the phenomenon of the Jewish kapos who were especially cruel to other Jews in Nazi concentration camps.

Note 132: Phyllis Schlafly is a woman who campaigned against the Equal Rights Amendment to the U.S. Constitution in the 1970s. She likes to tell the story of what a hoodwinked man believes. "When my wife and I were married," this foolish man says, "we agreed that I would make all the major decisions, and she would make the minor ones. I decide what legislation Congress should pass, what treaties the president should sign, and whether the United States should stay in the United Nations. My wife makes the minor decisions—such as how we spend our money, whether I should change my job, where we should live, and where we go on our vacations." Phyllis Schlafly. *The Power of the Positive Woman*. New Rochelle, NY: Arlington House. 1977.

Note 133: Boy-friendly writer Christina Hoff Sommers gives this example of men's failure to stand up for boys: "The move to eliminate recess [in schools] has aroused little notice and even less opposition…Girls benefit from recess—but boys absolutely need it…Needless to say, school officials today would never act in a manner equally dismissive of girls' characteristic desires and needs, for they know they would immediately face a storm of justified protests from women advocates. Boys have no such protectors." Christina Hoff Sommers. *The War Against Boys: How Misguided Feminism Is Harming Our Young Men*. New York: Touchstone. 2000. p. 95.

Note 134: George Vaillant is a psychiatrist and the director of the Harvard Study of Adult Development, the world's longest-running research of what makes men happy in life. When asked what he had learned, he replied, "That the only thing that really matters in life are your relationships to other people." [Joshua Wolf Shenk, "What Makes Us Happy?" *The Atlantic.* June 2009. p. 46.]

Note 135: Joseph Campbell. *The Hero's Journey: Joseph Campbell on His Life and Work.* Novato, CA: New World Library. 1990. p. 63 and p. 123.

Note 136: Rabbi Dan Moskovitz and Rabbi Perry Netter. *The Men's Seder: A Haggadah-based Exploration of Contemporary Men's Issues.* New York: Men of Reform Judaism. 2007.

Note 137: Jack Kammer. *Good Will Toward Men: Women Talk Candidly About the Balance of Power Between the Sexes.* New York: St. Martin's Press. 1994. This book is a collection of interviews with twenty-two male-friendly women, most of whom consider themselves feminists.

Note 138: Betty Friedan. "Their Turn: How Men Are Changing." *Redbook,* May 1980, p. 141. Betty Friedan is the woman who is often credited with starting modern feminism through her 1963 book, *The Feminine Mystique.*

Note 139: Gloria Steinem, *Revolution from Within: A Book of Self-Esteem.* Boston: Little, Brown and Co. 1992. p. 22. Gloria Steinem is one of the founders of *Ms. Magazine.*

Note 140: In 2007, men were 14 times as likely as women to be incarcerated in a state or federal prison. William J. Sabol and Heather Couture. U.S. Department of Justice, Bureau of Justice Statistics, Prison Inmates at Midyear 2007, NCJ 221944; Prisoners under state or federal jurisdiction, by selected characteristics, December 31, 2000 and 2006, and June 30, 2007. filename pim07t01.csv.

Note 141: While I did not see the program myself, the story has been related to me in personal conversations with Mr. Hayward and its essential facts have been corroborated by two persons who witnessed the live broadcast. I contacted the local station, WJZ-TV, in 2007 and was told that no transcript or videotape of that show is available.

Note 142: Esther Vilar, *The Manipulated Man.* London: Pinter & Martin Ltd. 2005, p 60. The book was written and first published in German as *Der Dressierte Mann* in 1971. It was published in English in 1972. In her Introduction to the 2005 edition, Vilar wrote, "I hadn't imagined broadly enough the isolation I would find myself in after writing this book. Nor had I envisaged the consequences which it would have for my subsequent writing and even for my private life—violent threats have not ceased to this date." p. 8.

Note 143: John Burnett, "Mexican Drug Cartels Recruiting Young Men, Boys," National Public Radio's "Morning Edition," March 24, 2009.

Note 144: Stan Grant, "Kidnapped Boys 'Brainwashed' to Die as Suicide Bombers." CNN. August 3, 2009.

Note 145: Cecil Adams, "The Straight Dope." December 19, 2008.

Note 146: The headmaster of a private all-male academy in Maryland told Christina Hoff Sommers that boys feel freer to do things when girls aren't around. Football players get excited about playing the choir chimes, for instance. [Christina Hoff Sommers. *The War Against Boys: How Misguided Feminism Is Harming Our Young Men*. New York: Touchstone. 2000, p. 175.]

Note 147: A boy who showed "dramatic improvement" at an all-boy school said, "I don't worry as much about what girls think." *US News & World Report*, July 30, 2001.

Note 148: There is credible evidence that the Obama administration intends to extend Title IX gender proportionality requirements from athletic departments to such academic departments as physics, engineering and math. (Christina Hoff Sommers. "A Threat in Title IX," *Washington Post*, April 14, 2009. p. A17.) Given the high rate of incarceration of American males, and given the challenges faced by young males in school, the national interest seems much more at stake in having gender balance in social work and early childhood education than in math, engineering and physics. If gender balance in math and physics is important, is it not important in nursing, dental hygiene, library science—and modern dance and art history, for that matter?

Note 149: On April 28, 2009 I was a guest on "The Secret Lives of Men," an Internet radio show hosted by psychologist Chris Blazina. Another guest was Keith E. Edwards, Director of Campus Life at Macalester College, who in his official capacity is involved with many campus discussions about sexual assault and coercion. After I offered the view that it would be helpful if college women were asked to acknowledge that they sometimes demean college men, that they sometimes objectify college men and dismiss their emotions, and that they sometimes use sex as a source of power, material acquisition and ego gratification, Dr. Edwards said four times during his three-minute response that my call for more candor was "particularly painful" to him. The good news is we ended up agreeing that helping college-age males secure more emotional and behavioral options, and providing you with more empathy, encouragement and support would be very good for your health and happiness.

Note 150: AVP Education Committee. Basic Course Manual. AVP/USA, St. Paul, Minnesota. 2002. See avpusa.org.

Bibliography

Biddulph, Steve. *Raising Boys: Why Boys Are Different, And How To Help Them Become Happy and Well-Balanced Men.* Lane Cove NSW Australia: Finch Publishing, 1998.

Cancian, Francesca M.; *Love in America: Gender and Self-Development*; Cambridge University Press, 1987.

Farrell, Warren. *Father and Child Reunion: How to Bring the Dads We Need to the Children We Love.* New York: Tarcher. 2001.

Farrell, Warren. *Why Men Earn More: The Startling Truth Behind the Pay Gap—and What Women Can Do About It.* New York: American Management Association/AMACOM, 2005.

Fisher, Helen. *Anatomy of Love.* New York: W.W. Norton, 1992.

Garbarino, James. *Lost Boys: Why Our Sons Turn Violent and How We Can Save Them.* New York: Free Press, 1999.

Goldberg, Herb. *The Hazards of Being Male: Surviving the Myth of Masculine Privilege.* New York: Signet, 1977.

Gurian, Michael. *The Wonder of Boys: What Parents, Mentors, and Educators Can Do to Shape Boys into Exceptional Men.* New York: Tarcher, 1997.

Gurian, Michael. *The Purpose of Boys: Helping Our Sons Find Meaning, Significance, and Direction in Their Lives.* San Francisco: Jossey-Bass, 2009.

Handel, Gerald (ed.). *Childhood Socialization.* Piscataway NJ: Aldine Transaction, 2005.

Harrison, Harry H., Jr. *Father to Son.* New York: Workman Publishing, 2000.

Kammer, Jack. *Good Will Toward Men: Women Talk Candidly About the Balance of Power Between the Sexes.* New York: St. Martin's Press, 1994. Republished 2007: www.RulyMob.com.

Keen, Sam. *Fire in the Belly: on Being a Man.* New York: Bantam, 1992.

Kimmel, Michael. *Guyland: The Perilous World Where Boys Become Men.* New York: HarperCollins, 2008.

Kindlon, Dan and Michael Thompson. *Raising Cain: Protecting the Emotional Life of Boys.* New York: Ballantine, 1999.

Kipnis, Aaron. *Knights Without Armor: A Practical Guide for Men in Quest of Masculine Soul.* Los Angeles: Tarcher, 1991.

Kiselica, Mark S., Matt Englar-Carlson and Arthur M. Horne (eds.). *Counseling Troubled Boys: A Guidebook for Professionals.* New York: Taylor & Francis Routledge, 2008.

Klaus, Marshall H. and John H. Kennell. *Maternal-Infant Bonding: The Impact of Early Separation or Loss on Family Development*. St. Louis: Moseby Press, 1976.

Lamb, Michael E. *The Role of the Father in Child Development*, Hoboken NJ: John Wiley & Sons, 2004.

Marx, Jeffrey. *Season of Life: A Football Star, a Boy, a Journey to Manhood*. New York: Simon & Schuster, 2003.

Mead, Margaret. *Sex and Temperament in Three Primitive Societies*. New York: Morrow, 1935.

Mills, Linda G. *Violent Partners: A Breakthrough Plan for Ending the Cycle of Abuse*. New York: Basic Books, 2008.

Mortola, Peter, Howard Hiton and Stephen Grant. *BAM! Boys Advocacy and Mentoring: A Leader's Guide to Facilitating Strengths-Based Groups for Boys*. New York: Routledge, 2008.

Moskovitz, Rabbi Dan and Rabbi Perry Netter. *The Men's Seder: A Haggadah-based Exploration of Contemporary Men's Issues*. New York: Men of Reform Judaism, 2007.

Pearson, Patricia. *When She Was Bad: Violent Women and the Myth of Innocence*. New York: Viking, 1997.

Pollack, William. *Real Boys: Rescuing Our Sons from the Myths of Boyhood*. New York: Henry Holt, 1998.

Pruett, Kyle D. *FatherNeed: Why Father Care Is as Essential as Mother Care for Your Child*. New York: Free Press, 2000.

Real, Terrence. *I Don't Want to Talk About It: Overcoming the Secret Legacy of Male Depression*. New York: Scribner, 1997.

Schlafly, Phyllis. *The Power of the Positive Woman*. New Rochelle, NY: Arlington House, 1977.

Sommers, Christina Hoff. *The War Against Boys: How Misguided Feminism Is Harming Our Young Men*. New York: Touchstone, 2000.

Stearns, Peter N. *Be a Man!: Males in Modern Society*. Teaneck, NJ: Holmes & Meier Publishers, 1979.

Steinem, Gloria. *Revolution from Within: A Book of Self-Esteem*. Boston: Little, Brown and Co, 1992.

Tyre, Peg. *The Trouble with Boys: A Surprising Report Card on Our Sons, Their Problems at School, and What Parents and Educators Must Do*. New York: Crown. 2008.

About the Author

When I was about your age I was pretty happy. I had brothers and sisters, a mother and father, lots of friends, I was doing well in school, I was fairly good at sports, though definitely not a super-star, and I enjoyed playing them. Life Was Good.

But I also remember some things that made me unhappy, things that didn't make sense, things that looked sad and scary.

Back in the 1960s, '70s and '80s, athletic girls often heard "You're really good at sports… for a girl." And girls who enjoyed working with numbers often heard, "You're really good at math… for a girl." When I was a boy I heard a different kind of left-handed compliment: "You're really good with babies… for a boy." It was clear to me even as a youngster that people were trying to tell me something about my rightful territory and about proper boy behavior that I refused to accept. What exactly were they trying to say? Whatever it was I knew I didn't like it.

I remember seeing fathers leave the house every morning and thinking how sad it was that they had to leave their babies and little children all day, every day. I didn't want that to be my life.

My father was a doctor. He worked long hours to care for his patients, but when he came home he was tired. And often grumpy. He became more and more of a stranger to his kids. And we became strangers to him. Since he made a lot of money, he was a Big Success. But I knew something was wrong. I felt sorry for him. He seemed quite pathetic as a stranger in his own house.

One of the best things I ever did in my entire life was deliver my father's eulogy: at his funeral in 1985 I honored his life and his memory—truthfully: he was a great doctor and, sadly for his seven kids, that meant he had little time or energy left over to be a great father.

When I kept hearing that "It's a man's world," I knew it didn't look like a man's world to me. Sure, there were some parts of being a man that looked good. But mostly it looked like a lot of tension and stress. I didn't see much joy in it.

When I was about twelve I noticed my male friends started acting different. They were showing off for each other, trying to put each other down. And showing off for the girls, too. It looked ugly. They reminded me of my father somehow. They could never relax. They seemed always worried about something. They were joyless. As I look back now I guess they were worried about not being men, about not being winners in a game that didn't seem worth playing.

In the 1980s I was in my 30s and playing on a co-ed softball team. After the games when we went out for drinks and dinner, some of the women on the team found they could talk easily with me, mainly because I'd listen. Often they'd want to talk about their "lousy" or "rotten" or "horrible" boyfriends. They'd tell me some story about what their men had done and then they'd say something like, "And so he's a real jerk. Don't you think?" I'd smile and say, "Well, maybe. But on the other hand maybe the way it looks to him is like this..." And I'd say something that made perfect sense to me and was almost totally obvious from my experience as a man. And each time the woman threw her hand over her gaping mouth and said, "Oh, my gosh! I never thought of that! That makes sense because just last week he said..."

So it began to be clear to me that women didn't understand the male point of view very well and that men weren't doing a very good job of explaining that male perspective. I've been writing and talking about what's going on with men and boys ever since. From 2005 to 2008 I earned two Masters Degrees, one in Business, the other in Social Work, so I could be in a better position to work on these issues that I care about so much.

I've never been married and I have no kids of my own. If you like this book I hope it's okay with you if I think of you as a nephew. Being an uncle is one of the greatest joys of my life. (It is also, I readily acknowledge, much easier than being a father.)

Jack Kammer, MSW, MBA is the director of the Center for Men and Boys in Social Policy, a public interest consultancy in Baltimore, Maryland USA. [believeinmen.com]

5660204R0

Made in the USA
Lexington, KY
03 June 2010